COLD KISS

AMY GARVEY

An Imprint of HarperCollinsPublishers

HarperTeen is an imprint of HarperCollins Publishers.

Cold Kiss

Copyright © 2011 by Amy Garvey

www.epicreads.com

Library of Congress Cataloging-in-Publication Data
Garvey, Amy, 1967-
    Cold kiss / Amy Garvey. — 1st ed.
        p.   cm.
    Summary: When her boyfriend is killed in a car accident, high
school student Wren Darby uses her hidden powers to bring him back
from the dead, never imagining the consequences that will result from
her decision.
    ISBN 978-0-06-199622-1
    [1. Future life—Fiction. 2. Psychic ability—Fiction. 3.
Dead—Fiction. 4. Interpersonal relations—Fiction. 5. High
schools—Fiction. 6. Schools—Fiction.] I. Title.
PZ7.G21172Co   2011   2010040421
[Fic]—dc22   CIP
                                                    AC

Typography by Torborg Davern
11   12   13   14   15   CG/BV   10 9 8 7 6 5 4 3 2 1
❖

First Edition

FOR STEPHEN, AS ALWAYS.

KEEP THE TEA AND CUPCAKES COMING, BABE.

PROLOGUE

I WASN'T THINKING ABOUT FALLING IN LOVE the day I met Danny Greer. I wasn't thinking about anything beyond the paper on the Industrial Revolution I hadn't yet started, and the cool pewter sky above me. I was lying on the top row of the bleachers facing the practice field, watching the clouds skid past, and absently wondering if I could lift myself off the cold metal. Just a few inches. Nothing anyone would notice.

There wasn't much chance of that anyway. A few people were hanging out on the lower rows, seniors mostly, passing around a Red Bull and wandering off to smoke in one of their cars. Out on the field Ms. Singer's fifth-period PE class was choosing up sides for soccer. No one was paying any attention to me, which suited me just fine.

Jess and Darcia had drawn sixth-period lunch, and I had lunch alone. I didn't mind being out here on the bleachers by myself, which was where I'd be every lunch period until it got too cold. By November I'd probably hole up in the library, hiding a yogurt from Mrs. Gaffney at the table way in the back, behind Technology and Applied Sciences. Until then I was happy to read the clouds and make the leaves dance in scuffling, twisting funnels along the curb.

Or lift myself off the bleachers, even though it hadn't worked so far.

I closed my eyes, concentrating, the ridges of the metal bench digging into my spine through my jacket. The wind had picked up, spreading the familiar scent of earth and dead leaves, but something else, too. Something heavier, thick, almost electric, like a storm in the distance.

I opened my eyes to find someone staring down at me, and almost toppled over.

"I thought you were asleep," the boy said, and straightened up.

"And you thought staring was a good idea?"

"You could have been dead," he offered with a shrug.

"You were doing a good imitation of a statue. Or, you know, a dead thing."

I blinked. With the weak autumn light behind him, I couldn't see much more than a rough outline of an angular face, and shaggy hair that fell into eyes deep in shadow.

I could just make out his mouth, though. It was wide, full, and right then it was twisted into a smile.

"Thank you," I said without thinking, and watched him bite his bottom lip. The electric thrill vibrating in the air was in my blood now, tingling, and for a moment I felt my spine hover over the metal. A breeze whistled between my back and the bench in the afterthought of space there.

"You're kind of weird," the boy said, but he was still smiling when he pushed my legs aside and sat down next to me.

That was Danny.

It wasn't love right away, because nothing ever is, no matter what the songs say, but it was the start of it. A beginning in one way, and the end in another. I think that might always be true of love.

We were completely different. Danny was tall, sweet, graceful despite legs that went on forever. I was little, moody, uncoordinated. We didn't like the same music or the same movies. He put onions and mushrooms on his pizza and never wore socks and could sleep through a pipe bomb. I survived on bananas and yogurt and always wore hats and got carsick unless I chewed gum with my headphones on.

It didn't matter. I loved him. I loved him so much that I couldn't see anything else for a while. Danny filled the cracks inside me, blotted out the cold, empty places in the world. It didn't take long before Danny was the only thing that mattered.

Love like that is what they make movies about. It's the thing you're supposed to want, the answer to every question, the song that you're supposed to sing.

But love like that can be too big, too. It can be something you shouldn't be trusted to hold when you're the kind of person who drops the eggs and breaks the remote control.

Love doesn't break easily, I found. But people do.

CHAPTER ONE

DANNY WAITS FOR ME IN THE LOFT ABOVE Mrs. Petrelli's garage. We've made a kind of nest there against the wall away from the broken window. Two ancient, sour mattresses are stacked in the corner, covered with an old striped sheet I took from my basement. There's a blanket, too, mostly for me, a wooden crate full of books and paper and colored pencils, a couple of pillows, and a box of fat white candles.

We don't see much of each other in the daylight.

Mrs. Petrelli's house is behind mine, and I cut through the ragged hedge that borders our yard to make my way to the garage. Mrs. Petrelli is that indeterminate kind of old—too ancient to work anymore, not that she ever did, as far as I know, but not frail enough to be carted off to a nursing home yet. When Mr. Petrelli died two years ago, she sort of deflated, curling in on herself like a yellowed piece of paper. She doesn't drive anymore, so she never bothers with her garage.

Danny's lying on the mattresses when I climb the wobbly pull-down stairs, but he sits up right away. In the darkness, it's startling to watch him, the slow, graceful rise of his upper body, his head turning so he can smile at me.

"You came." He sounds surprised, grateful, and the words twist in my chest, a tight little knot of guilt.

"I always do." I curl up beside him, laying my head on his shoulder. "I always will."

I shiver a little, pressing my cheek into his collarbone. It's getting harder to remember the way Danny used to be. That Danny wouldn't have waited so patiently for me. He would have called, snuck up behind me in the hall at school, and buried his face against my neck. That Danny had ideas, crazy, late-night fantasies strung together like a paper-clip chain. He was going to teach me to sing so I could join his band, and then we would go on the road. Ryan was going to be the one to finance our rock odyssey, even though Becker was the one with money, because Danny said Ryan was the one with the brains. Danny's charm got under your skin the way a good song got stuck in your head, and after a while you couldn't help humming it.

Then there was the comic strip idea. Danny had pages of drawings of me, and one day I found him redrawing them with broader strokes, bolder outlines, exaggerating my pointed chin and the way my hair spiked up in the front. I thought I looked like a sullen baby chick, but he just shook his head and pulled me onto his lap. "You're going to be a superhero. It'll be awesome. Trust me."

And I did, even though I growled at the picture of me climbing onto a table to shoot actual daggers out of my eyes at a vampire that looked a lot like one of the PE teachers at school. I was short, yeah, but it didn't need to be emphasized. I elbowed him in the side for that. He just laughed.

I trusted Danny with everything, even when he was pulling me up a fire escape in the middle of the night to get to the roof above the movie theater, where you could follow the dark, lazy curves of the train tracks as they headed toward the city. I let him feed me spicy curry for the first time and kiss the heat out of my mouth. I watched in the mirror when he cut my hair one long, sultry afternoon, holding up the fuzzy ends and shaking his head.

And I'd given all of myself in return. Almost, anyway. The one thing I'd kept secret was the only reason he was here now.

"I brought you some more paper." I hand him the drawing tablets I'd bought at the dollar store after school. They're cheap, flimsy, intended for little kids to use with fat crayons and finger paint, but I know he won't care. I could bring him used candy wrappers and wrinkled pieces of the Sunday paper and he would beam at me.

"I needed some." He doesn't look at them, though, just lays them behind him on the bed, and leans in, resting his forehead against mine, the way he has so many times, both then and now. "Thank you."

I know what he wants, and it wasn't so long ago that he wouldn't have had to ask, when I would have climbed into his lap instead of just sitting beside him. Back then, we were attached at the mouth whenever possible.

It's different now. I didn't expect it to be. My mom says I was always that kid, the one who learns the hard way about the glowing red burner on the stove and just how high the monkey bars are when you're falling from them into the damp wood chips on the playground.

I tilt my head up, my mouth brushing his lightly, and he pulls me closer. "Missed you," he murmurs, lips against my cheek after a second. "Always miss you."

When he finally kisses me, really kisses me, his lips are cool and dry and his arms are tight around me, fingers of one hand tangled in my hair. He tastes like smoke and ashes, the bitter weight of wet earth, but I kiss him back, my palm resting on his cheek.

"Always want you." The words are breathed against my mouth, and I relax into the circle of his arms as he pulls me closer. He'll stop when I tell him to—he'll do anything I tell him to now—but I never say no to kissing.

I have so little to give him. I hadn't considered that—I thought I was giving him everything he could ever want that July night, candlelight hot beneath my palms as I chanted. For once, I didn't think I was being selfish.

I'm wrong a lot. Anyone will tell you.

Anyway, I miss it, the kissing, the comfortable weight of his arm around my shoulders as we walked home from school, the clean smell of his sweat after he'd been playing guitar with Becker and Ryan in Becker's basement, all warm, musky boy. I miss him, too, when I'm away from him all day.

"You remember the first time?" he says. He's laying me down, and the sheet is cold through my sweater, slightly damp in the October night air. His hands are even cooler, smooth and solid as marble, and I shiver when he runs a finger over my cheekbone. "Remember when you kissed me?"

He asks me things like this all the time now. The first movie we went to (a terrible horror movie that made me laugh so hard, I choked on a piece of popcorn), the first time I met his parents (a Friday in late December, in the close, overheated crush of the drugstore, where everyone was buying bows and foil-wrapped chocolate Santas), the song that was playing on my iPod the first time he called me (the Brobecks' "Visitation of the Ghost").

He likes it when I tell him the stories out loud, and goes still as he listens—too still, silent. His eyes are the only things that move, watching my face, my mouth, as if he's trying to picture what happened so he can hold on to the memories.

I worry that he's trying to remember what those moments felt like, what *he* felt like then. One day he's going to understand that he's not that boy anymore.

"It was three weeks after we met," I tell him, whispering even though no one can hear us way up here. I twine my fingers in his, holding tight. Even now, his hand is familiar, huge around mine, the long bones of his fingers sturdy. "We were outside the library, and it was almost dark and really cold. You put your algebra book down on the ledge so you could wrap your scarf around my neck, and I grabbed your hands and pulled you down and kissed you. Right in front of Tommy Gellar and that freak cheerleader he was sleeping with."

It's not romantic the way I tell it, but Danny smiles anyway, and the hard focus in his eyes softens. "You tasted like Juicy Fruit," he says, and rests his forehead against mine. "I remember that."

I do, too. I remember so much more than I tell him, because it makes me hot and uncomfortable to say some things out loud, even now. There was the way I could feel the length of his thigh against mine while we went over his tragic attempt at explaining the symbolism in *The Glass Menagerie*. The warm, sort of spicy smell of him in his layered T-shirts. The electric hum beneath my skin when he leaned close to ask me a question and his breath whispered over my cheek.

If I'd wanted to, I could have lifted right out of my chair and touched the ceiling that night, just sitting beside him in the library. And when I kissed him, opened my mouth to taste him, I shut my eyes to find the darkness melted into old gold.

I still have that scarf, tucked away in a torn cardboard box under my bed.

"I would have kissed you, you know," he says, and slides his palm along my ribs, ticking off each one with his thumb. "If you hadn't kissed me first."

I believe him. But in the end, it doesn't really matter. I've always been a step ahead of him, even when I don't know where I'm going, or where I might take him.

The house is dark when I let myself in the back door. It's almost eleven, a school night, and Robin's probably up in her room talking on the phone. I cross through the kitchen and glance into the living room, where my mom is curled on the sofa, lights out and the blue glare of the TV flickering over her face. I freeze for a second—she's usually asleep by now these days, at least since she broke up with Tom.

Her boyfriends never last long. I wonder if they get discouraged when they see the picture of my dad on the mantel. Even though he's been gone for ten years, that picture never moves. Mom says it's there for Robin and me, but I see her looking at it, too.

Memories of Dad are what I couldn't bear to have Danny become—a faded, flickering impression of a stubbled cheek scratching my face when he hugged me, the pine scent of aftershave, the low rumble of his laugh.

"Wren?"

I turn around before she can lift her head, pretending to be heading for the kitchen instead of away from it. I skin off my jacket and toss it toward the tiny stairwell leading down to the basement as she sits up.

"Just getting something to drink," I say, and head into the kitchen without waiting to see if she'll follow. I'm taking a diet soda out of the fridge when she pads in, yawning and pushing her hair out of her face.

She kisses the back of my head, and I close my eyes, waiting for her to say something. I can still feel the night chill on my clothes, on my skin, but as far as my mother knows I've been up in my room all night.

She pulls away, though, and fills the teakettle with water. I lean against the fridge with my soda, hoping she won't notice if I don't open it.

My mom is good at seeing only what she wants to see. About men, about the hair salon she owns, which only crosses the line into profitable once in a while, about the condition of our house, which she's decided "has character," since that sounds better than "falling down." Right now I'm pretty sure she doesn't want to think about why I might have been out of the house tonight, although I know she can tell I have been. She doesn't always like to examine things too closely, but she's not stupid.

"Want some tea?" she says so suddenly that I jump. She's looking right at me now, and my heart is beating too loud, a steady bass-drum *thump* beneath my T-shirt and black hoodie. She sets the kettle on the burner, and it flares to life before she can even reach the knob, which is bad news. Mom doesn't usually let me see her do things like that.

"No, thanks," I say, trying to keep my voice steady. Tea means sitting at the kitchen table together in the dark, talking, and I can't do that tonight. I can't do that at all anymore, not with Mom, because when she wants to, the one thing she can see right into, down to bone and blood, is me. "I'm going to go to bed, I guess. I have a chemistry test tomorrow."

There's nothing more than weak moonlight filtered through the window over the sink, and the faint yellow glow of a night-light in the baseboard on the wall behind me, but even so I can see the betrayal in Mom's eyes. She knows I'm lying, not about the test or the tea, but about something.

The blue flame licks higher at the scorched bottom of the kettle, just for a second, hungry and hot, and then she looks away to take a mug down from the cupboard. "All right, babe. Sleep well."

I'm careful not to slam the door to my room, but when I get inside, I let the harsh buzz gathered just beneath my skin flicker out, a quick electric jolt that knocks the pile of books off my desk. *Basic Principles of Chemistry* falls hardest, pages crushed under its open spine, and I stare at it for a minute. I'm panting, my heart still tripping crazily, and instead of picking it up, I step around it to flop on my bed, a tangle of sheets and blue-striped comforter and clothes.

Across the room, Danny smiles down at me from a framed picture on my dresser. He was being extra goofy that day, making faces at Ryan's camera as we all hung out on Becker's front porch, stealing Ryan's baseball cap and crossing his eyes as he pushed the porch swing into motion with one long bare foot.

"Point that thing at Wren, you loser," he'd said, throwing a pretzel across the porch at Ryan to get his attention. "She's the only one worth looking at."

In that picture, which Ryan printed out for me a week later, Danny's mouth is tilted up on one side in the little smile that was just for me. His whole face softened when he smiled that way, like he'd just remembered this incredible secret.

Some days now I can't look at it. The frame spends a lot of time buried in the bottom drawer with my jeans, because it's the same smile Danny gives me whenever I climb into the loft. Like nothing's changed. Like I'm *his* secret, and there's nothing he'd rather see than my face.

Sometimes when he sits up to look at me, or when I walk into my room and catch a glimpse of that picture, it's all I can do not to scream. Scream and scream until my throat is shredded and every window shatters and the room goes up in flames.

I've only set something on fire once. It was one of Danny's T-shirts, actually, an ancient gray Clash shirt his sister scored on eBay for his birthday. I'd found it on my bedroom floor right before Ryan called, and I was twisting it in one fist by the time he told me Becker was in the hospital and Danny was dead.

It hissed and sputtered for a second before a hot, angry tongue licked out and burned my wrist. I dropped it on the floor, and the phone with it. Ryan was still talking, a tiny, distant voice.

I don't remember a lot of what happened after that, but the scorch mark is still there, a sooty black circle against the faded oak. Mom's not sure it will ever come out completely, but she never once asked me how it got there.

CHAPTER TWO

I WASN'T EVEN THIRTEEN YET THE FIRST TIME. It reminded me of a sneeze coming on, that tingling tension when you know it's going to happen and you can't stop it. But this feeling was bigger than that, a vibrating hum just beneath my skin that made me squirm all over.

I was mad at my mother, which was pretty much a daily thing back then. She'd said no to a sleepover at Darcia's because I hadn't finished my social studies project, and in her words, "There's no way I'm going to listen to you whine about it all day tomorrow, when you're rushing to get it done."

Robin stuck her tongue out at me from across the

kitchen table, and I made a face at her before I stood up. "Clear your place, Wren," my mother said, not bothering to glance over her shoulder as she rinsed dishes in the sink.

I didn't even have a chance to mutter, "Do I ever forget?" because the humming was louder now, a hot, angry itch just beneath my skin, and then the lightbulb in the fixture over the kitchen table hissed and exploded in a white arc.

Robin screamed and waved her arms, batting at her hair, brittle pieces of glass skittering over the table, until my mother cut through the noise. "Stop it! Just sit still."

I had frozen in place, my plate still in my hands, my mouth hanging open. The weird buzz had subsided, leaving behind a kind of dull sting, like the last day of a bad sunburn, but the kitchen was still crackling with electricity.

This, I was pretty sure, was one of those Things We Didn't Talk About. Like where our dad was or why Mom didn't invite Aunt Mari to the house anymore.

Or why, sometimes, even when the electric got shut off because Mom was behind on the bills, she could disappear into the basement and the lights would flare to life. Mom had broken her share of lightbulbs, and once the mirror over the bathroom sink, which cut us all in half diagonally for months before she replaced it.

She could make other things happen, too, better things. Balloons that stayed afloat for days after Robin's birthday party. Daffodils that budded long before anyone else's. A fire in the fireplace that burned for hours on just a handful of newspaper and a stray twig.

When I was really little, six or seven, and Dad had just left, I woke up crying almost every night, shrugging off nightmares like a tangled net. Mom would get into bed with me and sing, low, nonsense tunes that she said Gram had sung to her when she was a kid. And above me, the ceiling would swirl with gently sparkling lights, like summer fireflies, flickering in and out with the tune.

Those moments were gifts, offered freely, as surprising and wonderful as unexpected gifts always are, unlike the broken mirror and, once, the smoking ruin of the backyard. But even the fairy lights and the balloons weren't something Robin or I could ask about. The warning was always there in Mom's eyes, a monster in the closet of a brightly lit room.

Mom had never once mentioned it would happen to me, too, even though I knew Aunt Mari and Gram could do the same things. It seemed like one of those grown-up privileges, I guess, and not one Mom approved of anymore. But when Robin and I were little, she was totally free about it, and so were Gram and Aunt Mari.

I remember one Christmas when Robin was really little, not even two, and Gram had taken me into the backyard with Dad. It was snowing, fat, lacy flakes swirling out of the sky, and the trees were dripping with icicles from the night before. Gram stood there wrapped in her big red coat as Dad and I caught snowflakes on our tongues, and she lit up all the icicles like Christmas lights with just a few whispered words.

Dad had grinned, his teeth as white as the blanket of snow on the grass. "Nicely done, Rowan," he said, and kissed her cheek. It was too cold to stay out much longer, but I held on to that moment after Dad was gone and later, when Gram died. What I couldn't understand was what could be bad about something like that, something that was pure beauty, and why Mom never wanted to talk about it.

Even that night when I shattered the lightbulb, and she was picking sheer slivers of glass out of Robin's hair, she didn't say a word. Just tightened her mouth into a hard line and told me to get the broom.

Instead, I set my plate down on the table with a hollow *thud* and ran upstairs to my room.

It's different now. Aunt Mari has told me some of it, even though Mom would probably kill us both if she knew.

But once I was old enough to walk downtown on my own, I figured nothing was stopping me from going to Aunt Mari's apartment or meeting her at Bliss, the coffee shop where I work now. Whatever happened to change things after Dad was gone was the one thing Aunt Mari wouldn't talk to me about, but she was happy to share what she knew about the power inside of us.

Practice makes a big difference, too, even if I still can't levitate on my own. But once, when Danny and I were tangled on his bed making out, I had to pull away before he noticed I was hovering over him, a half-inch of space between us everywhere but our mouths.

Being with Danny focused whatever it was inside me, somehow. When we were together, holding hands or kissing or even just curled on the couch, that hum was much stronger, a constant pulse I could feel hot in my blood. But I never showed him what I could do. I never once hinted at it. Even without Aunt Mari's warnings and a lifetime of my mother's example, I knew the things I could make happen were just for me.

Even now, Danny doesn't know what I am, or what I can do. But then, there are a lot of things Danny doesn't understand now.

The fact that I go to school without him is the worst, for him anyway. He doesn't miss classes, he just hates the fact that I can't stay with him all day, curled up in the loft. Last week, I stopped climbing up to see him on my way to school because I couldn't face having the same conversation over and over again.

"Why can't I come?" he would say, crowding me against the wall, as tall as ever, his cold hands cradling my face. "I miss you when you're not here. I'd just sit with you, Wren, I swear. I wouldn't get in the way. Quiet as a mouse, promise."

It's so hard to say no to that voice. Danny's always been pretty persuasive, and when he drops his voice like that, low and soft as he whispers against my cheek, I have to fight not to melt into a sloppy puddle.

What's worse is how much he sometimes sounds like the old Danny, the one who could make me laugh at all the wrong times, the one who could do dead-on impressions of Mrs. DiFranco intoning the morning announcements over the loudspeaker or ramble movie dialogue off the top of his head. My Danny, the one who died three months ago, is still in there, buried underneath the new one.

The one who doesn't want or think about anything but me.

CHAPTER THREE

I SHOULDER MY BACKPACK AND GO OUT THE
front door when I leave the house this morning, the way
I always do, but I can't help sinking down into the collar
of my jacket. There's no way Danny can see me from the
one window in the garage loft, but I'm always worried
that he's watching anyway.

I look over my shoulder a dozen times as I walk to
school. As far as I know, he has to do what I tell him to
do, and even when he argues about it, which isn't often,
he's never once actually ignored me. I'm not sure he can,
but the last thing I need is to find him shambling along
behind me, pale and squinting in the sharp October sun,

calling my name.

Once I'm at school, lockers slamming and kids laughing and shouting at one another down the hall, I can relax. I slide into my seat in homeroom and nod at Meg D'Angelo, who still has her iPod earbuds in. She nods back, same way she does every morning—we've known each other since third grade, and she's one of those sort-of friends, someone I hang out with at school when Jess and Darcia aren't around.

Of course, I haven't seen them much since Danny died in July, and while Jess has gotten angrily vocal about it over the last few weeks, Darcia just stares at me sadly across the row that separates us in World Lit and sends me cryptic texts about new songs she likes or her little brother's soccer games.

At least Meg doesn't look at me like I've disappointed her.

I slouch down to get my French notebook out of my backpack while Mr. Rokozny calls roll. Madame Hobart is quizzing us on the imperfect tense today, and I fell asleep watching a rerun of some reality show before I even thought about studying.

I raise my hand silently when Mr. Rokozny calls my name, and it's only when he pauses after Cleo Darnell's name to say, "Gabriel DeMarnes?" that I look up.

Twenty-two pairs of eyes are trained on the kid in the very back of the room. Even Rokozny is squinting at him from above the morning's roll. This far into October, it's weird to find a new kid in homeroom.

"That's me," the boy says, and Audrey Diehl sits up a little straighter, head tilted in appreciation.

He's tall—I can tell even though he's hunched over his desk, because his long legs stick out into the faded linoleum of the aisle. His hair is the color of clean sand, and even short it's sort of messy. He's all angles, planes, a geometry proof of a boy in a wrinkled yellow button-down and faded jeans, and when I drag my gaze away from the long, slender fingers splayed loose over his thigh, I blink in surprise.

Because even with everyone in the room checking him out, he's staring right at me.

Gabriel DeMarnes is everywhere that day, like a bad smell. Gabriel DeMarnes and his odd gray-blue eyes, which are focused on me way too often.

He takes the empty seat beside me in trig, dropping the battered textbook Ms. Nardini gives him on the desk with a *thud*. He has a notebook and a single pencil, but he doesn't touch either one of them. Whenever he's not pretending to listen to Ms. Nardini ramble on about ratio identity, he's looking at me out of the corner of his eye.

It makes me itchy in all the wrong ways, heart beating too fast and too hard, like a rabbit, and a dangerous electric tension humming under my skin. He's making me nervous, which is making me angry, because he's just a *boy*, a stupid new boy who doesn't know anyone and is probably fascinated by something equally stupid, like my beat-up purple Chucks or the fading black heart Danny drew in Sharpie on the back of my left hand two days ago.

But the sixth time I manage to turn my head and actually catch him staring, it's obvious that he's not looking at any of that. He's looking at *me*, and somehow he's seeing past what I've got on, past my hair and the trio of silver hoops in my right ear.

Except it's more than that. Even though I haven't said a word to him, he looks like he's *listening* to me. His head is tilted to one side, and he's concentrating, squinting a little bit, like he's trying to catch something he can't quite hear, and the loose end of that coiled electricity snaps rough over my nerves.

"What?" I hiss, and the globe at the front of the room falls off its stand with a crash.

I swallow hard and fix my eyes on my desk as Ms. Nardini gasps in surprise. "Okay, well, that was weird," she says with a nervous laugh. She's pretty much fresh out of college, where she was a sorority girl if the rumors are true, and she always follows her lesson plan like she's got a gun to her head.

She's still examining the globe for cracks when I sneak a glance at Gabriel.

He's smiling.

By the time he walks into history during seventh period, I'm seething. That makes three classes we have together, not counting homeroom. Three hours of him watching me, head tilted, hair flopping over his forehead and hiding his cool eyes when I glance at him.

I prop my head in my hand, doing my best to keep the furious simmer of energy inside me under control. So far the only other casualty has been a lightbulb in Madame Hobart's French classroom, but it's getting harder to ignore that hum. My free hand twitches into a fist on my lap, nails digging into my palm, and the sting slices through the urge to let that current roll up out of me and explode.

If Mr. Dorsey gives homework, I have no idea what it is. I'm the first one out of the room when the bell rings.

Darcia's waiting when I walk into World Lit, chewing on a hank of her dark hair, her feet propped on her seat and one arm wrapped around her knees.

"Did you finish the reading?"

"I skimmed," I say, and drop into my chair. If Gabriel walks into this class, I'm going to have to throw myself on Darcia to make sure she's not hit by the shrapnel.

She doesn't say anything until I've dug my notebook out of my backpack. When I look up, she's curling the ends of her hair around one finger. "Want to come over after school? We could work on the paper together."

For a minute, I let myself imagine it. Me and Darcia, the way we used to be, maybe Jess, too, scuffing through the leaves on the way to Darcia's house, Jess smoking her Marlboros and Darcia readjusting her stuffed backpack every few steps. The comfortable mess of Darcia's room, cans of diet Coke cracked open, and a half-empty bag of pretzels passed among us as Darcia organizes her homework and Jess sprawls on the bed, flipping through a magazine.

I want it so much, my heart thuds painfully. It's been too long since we just hung out the way we used to, and I know Darcia doesn't understand it—even when Danny was alive, I didn't abandon them, not completely, the way some girls do as soon as they have a boyfriend.

But then I see Danny in my head, sitting at the top of the stairs to the loft, restless, pale, jiggling one knee, and

I swallow hard. "The paper's not due for a week," I tell her, and turn back to my notebook just as Mrs. Garcia walks in.

When the bell rings and Gabriel is a no-show, I'm so relieved I pretend I don't notice Darcia's disappointment.

CHAPTER FOUR

JESS IS WAITING BY MY LOCKER AFTER SCHOOL, arms folded over her chest. Her dark blond hair is twisted up in a clip behind her head, and her jaw is set in a hard line. I thought I'd waited long enough to avoid her and Darcia both, but Jess is a little scary when she sets her mind to something. She pushed Billy Lanigan her first day at school when he knocked my lunch bag out of my hands, and that was third grade. Billy was twice her size.

"Are you going through, like, some hermit phase I didn't know about?" she says without even a simple hello. "Because it's getting really old."

I twist the dial on my lock, staring straight ahead. What am I supposed to say? I'm sorry? Again?

"I don't remember asking what you thought of it," I say instead. It sounds even worse out loud than it did in the millisecond before it fell out of my mouth, and Jess blinks at me.

"What the hell is wrong with you, Wren? What did we do to you? Actually, fuck that, what did Darcia do? Because I know *I* never did anything to deserve getting blown off like this."

When I look up at her, I swallow hard. She's furious, cheeks bright pink, eyes silvered with tears. That's wrong on every level. Jess doesn't cry. Jess just gets *mad*.

I drop my French book in surprise, and it thuds to the floor between her sleek black boots and my purple Chucks. For a second I just stare at it—the hum is back, a confused, buzzing swarm just under my skin, and if I move, if I speak, I'm afraid of what will happen.

"Fine," Jess says into the silence a moment later, and huffs out something that's too rough and ugly to be a laugh. "Whatever, Wren. Just . . . say something to Darcia, okay? She misses you."

She walks off, heels clicking angrily on the old linoleum, and for a second I'm frozen in place, staring at my French book, listening to the sound of her footsteps.

I could follow her. I could drop my backpack on the floor and pound down the hall to catch up. I could tell her I'm sorry. I could tell her I miss her and Darcia, too. I could tell her I'm stupid and awful and I suck.

It's all true.

But I can't tell her that my dead boyfriend is living in the neighbor's garage. I can't tell her I'm the one who brought him back. I can't tell her that I'm starting to wonder what's going to happen to him, and to me. He can't live there forever. He's not *living* in the first place.

That's all true, too, and I feel sick suddenly, my stomach tightening up like a fist. I grabbed Danny back because I couldn't stand to lose anything else, not when Dad was gone, and Gram was dead, and Aunt Mari was someone I had to see in secret. And now I'm losing Jess and Darcia, too.

I slide to the floor and sit with my back up against the lockers. The floor smells like old lemon wax and dust and feet, but I sit there until Mrs. Griffith wanders by and stops to ask me what's wrong.

By then, Jess is long gone.

It's already four when I finally leave, and even though I can imagine Danny pacing back and forth—or even scarier, sitting completely still at the top of the stairs, eyes fixed on the bottom, waiting for me—I walk through town to the library.

It's cold and gray out, and dead leaves swirl in rusty little clouds at my feet as I scuff up the sidewalk to the building. A couple of cheerleaders, seniors, are perched on the banister that lines the steps, blowing smoke rings and laughing. They ignore me, as usual, which has always been fine.

For the first time, though, it's tempting to turn around and focus, to pull whatever it is that's inside me into a tight glowing ball, and blow a nasty little kiss that would knock them over. Instead, I simply step on the hot pink strap of one of their backpacks as I run up the steps.

Inside, I head right to the 130s in the stacks. No one's ever in this particular aisle—I guess no one really cares about metaphysics or Western philosophy anymore, if they ever did in this town. I'm still not sure who decided the paranormal should be sandwiched between them, but whatever. That's what I need—information on the paranormal, emphasis on "para." I always knew I wasn't totally normal, but it's a little weird to see it right there in print, you know?

It always makes me wonder which part of me would pass if they gave a test.

There's nothing new on the shelves, and for a minute

I just stand there, my backpack heavy on one shoulder and the dusty, unused smell of the books in their plastic covers strong in my nose. Across the aisle, three middle-school boys are spread out at a table, flipping through old copies of *Maxim*, and story time is starting in the children's section—I can hear Mrs. Hodge shushing the kids. It's mostly quiet and a little too warm, and so overwhelmingly ordinary I want to scream.

How am I supposed to figure out what to do about Danny here? The books on the shelves lean more toward histories of the Salem witch trials than anything practical, except for a few books on Wicca, which have more to do with worshipping the Goddess than how to keep from shattering lightbulbs. At any rate, I have books at home that are more specific about spells and the craft, even if they don't tell me why I can do what I do, or how to control it better.

Or not to do certain things at all, even if the spell is right there.

I don't even know if there's a word for what I am, what the women in my family are. I asked Aunt Mari about it once, about a year ago.

"You know how electricity is just out there?" she'd said. She was lying on her back, staring at the ceiling as if the answers were written up there in the dingy off-white paint. "But to use it, you have to know how to harness it? That's what this is like. What we are. What we can do. Just like some musical prodigy can play Mozart at age three or whatever, we can tap into a kind of energy that other people can't. That's all."

That's all. Like it's no big deal that my mother can make flowers grow, and Mari can change the color of her hair at will, and I can (almost) lift myself off the ground and set things on fire. And, you know, raise my boyfriend from the dead.

Mari practically jumped up and down the first time she saw me make my old stuffed penguin dance, like it was this huge achievement. But I never told her when I started seriously experimenting with my power on my own. The whole subject was so off-limits, it felt like the one thing I had to hide from everyone. And I was trying things a little more complicated than making a pencil spin on my desk, or making the pale yellow daffodils hot pink.

Once I made it rain in Robin's bedroom, right over a pile of her dirty sweatshirts and socks. Another time I folded a piece of white lined paper into the shape of a bird and brought it to life. I was so terrified, I opened the window and let it go, once it had stopped flapping around my room in panic.

You'd think I would have learned my lesson.

I can't tell Aunt Mari about Danny. I can't tell anyone.

Standing in the library now, I can see him in my head, setting his jaw, starting down the stairs, and my pulse kicks so hard, a loose book on the edge of the shelf hits the floor. The kids across the aisle look up at me, and I glare until they shrink down into their sweatshirts and hold up their magazines again.

I'm not going to find anything here. I'm not even sure what I'm looking for anymore, and suddenly it's so hot, so close, I'm starting to sweat. I stumble past the kids and the ancient reference librarian, who frowns at me from behind his thick black plastic glasses, and out the door into the shockingly cool air.

Where I walk right into the one person I really don't want to see.

"Whoa, sorry," Gabriel says, catching me with both hands on my upper arms. "I didn't see you coming."

I'm positive he's lying. "Yeah, well." I shrug him off and start walking, but I can hear him following me, feet heavy on the sidewalk. I scan the quiet street and run across it, toward home.

"You don't like me," he says as he falls into step beside me, dry leaves and grass crackling underfoot. It's not a question.

"I don't know you." It's true, even if what he said is true, too.

"Gabriel," he says, and turns around to walk backward, holding out his hand. "Nice to meet you."

"God, what is your problem?" I'm trying for casual, dismissive, but my face is already hot, and I know he can see it. "Go find some other girl to bother. Believe me, they'll all be thrilled to have fresh meat to chew on."

"Not interested," he says, and steps easily over a dead twig, still walking backward, eyes fixed on my face.

"Not my problem," I tell him, and try to ignore the way my heart is pounding again. I can control myself, I *can*, I just have to concentrate. I walk faster, trying to pass him, but he matches me step for step.

"I can feel it, you know," he says, and suddenly stops dead, grabbing my arm so I stumble to a halt beside him. "What's inside you."

My blood is racing so hot through my veins, my skin is tight, tingling. He can't *know*, no one knows, it's not something you can see.

"I don't know what you're talking about," I manage, even though my tongue feels too thick in my mouth, huge and clumsy.

I break into a run before I'm even conscious that my

feet are moving, and all I can hear over my thudding footsteps is him calling, "Yes, you do."

I run right past my house, through the overgrown yard to Mrs. Petrelli's garage. I'm sweating, panting, completely out of breath, my backpack banging against one hip, but I don't care. I scramble up the stairs, and all I can think about is Danny holding me.

He's waiting, tense and blinking, standing at the edge of the makeshift bed. "Wren."

I don't—can't—say anything, I just drop my backpack with a thud on the dusty floor and walk into his arms, burying my head against his chest.

His arms tighten around me, fingers tangling in my hair. "I heard you coming. I missed you," he whispers, and sits down, pulling me into his lap.

He leans his cheek on my head, runs his hands down my spine and then back up, underneath my hoodie, and it's just like the million other times we've sat together like this.

It's what I wanted, but it's all wrong. He's cold and white as a bone, too hard, and when I lay my cheek against his chest, the silence is awful. I used to lie with him on the sofa in Becker's basement, or upstairs in my bed when Mom wasn't home, and count his heartbeats, a sturdy *thump-thump* I could feel beneath my palm, even through his T-shirt.

"What's wrong?" he says. "You're shaking."

There's no way to answer him. Not honestly, anyway. *You're wrong*, I want to say. *This is wrong. I was so, so wrong to think I could do this. Or hide it.*

Instead, I simply whisper, "Cold."

He holds me tighter, strokes my back. It doesn't make me any warmer, but I sit there anyway until it's dark, because he likes me there. He always seems more centered as soon as I come up to the loft. Whenever I manage to get up the stairs without him hearing me coming, he's sprawled so loosely on the bed that he looks a little bit like a marionette whose puppeteer has tossed him aside.

I can't run from this. I can't hide from him. Not in the library, not anywhere.

What's just as scary is that I guess I can't hide from Gabriel, either.

CHAPTER FIVE

PEOPLE ALWAYS SAY THEY FEEL NUMB AND empty when they lose someone.

I feel that way now sometimes, when Danny and I are curled together on his bed in the loft. But in the days right after he died? At his funeral? I felt like I'd been stuck under a glass, so that everything inside me—rage, grief, terror—resonated louder, harder, clanging together until I could feel it in my bones.

As we stood there beside his grave, the only sound other than the minister talking about eternal peace was Danny's mother, sobbing. Danny's dad had his arm around her, holding her up, but his jaw was clenched so tightly, I was pretty sure he was going to lose it any minute.

We all just stood there, our heads bowed and hands folded, listening, waiting for it to be over. Nothing was right—instead of gray and rainy, the way it was supposed to be, the way it always is in movies, it was a bright, hot July day. The sun poured through the leaves of the giant maple beside the plot.

But at Danny's grave that day I thought the crowd of football players and the stoners from his art class were probably glad they had a legitimate reason for their sunglasses, even though everyone knew they would have worn them anyway. It was hard not to choke up when you heard Danny's mom and little sister, Molly, sobbing, when you saw his older brother, Adam, choking back tears as their dad patted his back. None of us were supposed to die. Life was supposed to be what we were waiting for, not something already over.

When someone's cell went off a few feet behind us, my head went up so fast, I nearly lost my balance. My mother put a hand on my shoulder. I wanted to shrug it off, but I couldn't—any minute that glass around me was going to shatter, and all that furious energy was going to explode out of me. I had to shut my eyes for a second, trying not to imagine the carefully manicured lawn around the pit of Danny's grave going up in flames, or a sudden wind ripping through the cemetery, hurling the mourners against the headstones.

I couldn't let that happen, not to Danny's parents, and Ryan, and Danny's other real friends. Not even to Danny, although I knew that the boy I loved wasn't really in that casket. Not the part that mattered, anyway.

At home later, I went down to the basement. I figured I could do the least damage there—or maybe the most, without consequences anyway. Getting through the reception at Danny's house had taken more self-control than I thought it would, even though I hadn't managed to do much more than stand against the wall in the living room with a paper cup of punch in one hand, nodding at the people who came over to hug me.

I didn't even change my clothes before I ran down the basement steps, and I had fistfuls of my black shirt in each hand as I stared at the accumulated junk that we had let pile up over the years.

I had no idea what I expected to do. What I wanted was to blow a hole in the sky, explode a star, let the burning embers scorch me and everything they touched.

I jumped when my mother's hand landed on my shoulder again, warm and firm. She rested one palm against my cheek and handed me a chipped dish from a pile on a shelf. "Go on," she said. "It works just as well."

I stared at her, not understanding, every vein throbbing with the need to let all that energy out. But that wasn't what she meant. She picked up another—a cracked bowl from a set of green-striped dishes we used when I was really little—and smashed it against the dull gray cement floor.

I jumped again as the sound of it echoed inside me, and then I let the dish in my hand drop. It crashed among the broken shards of the bowl, pale blue pieces as sharp as the noise.

"Harder," Mom said, and handed me a mug without a handle. FIRST NATIONAL SAVINGS BANK was printed neatly around it in bright red letters. I hurled it at the bare spot on the wall beside the dryer, and it shattered so violently, pieces of it bounced over the floor to land between our feet.

In fifteen minutes we managed to break every old piece of dishware down there, until the floor was a jagged carpet of smashed pottery. When there was nothing left to throw, I sank to my knees and started to cry, the kind of huge, gulping, embarrassing sobs that make you blotchy and shaky. Mom settled down beside me, pulling me into her body until my face was pressed against her shoulder, and I had to wonder if she'd thrown things when Dad left, if she'd felt this alone and helpless.

I felt better afterward. Not right, not good, but not tied up in so many emotions I couldn't untangle them all.

There was a lesson there, I realized later. I didn't learn it, though.

"What are you thinking about?"

It's almost eleven, and Danny and I are lying on his bed, legs tangled together under an old blanket. I had to wait till Mom was asleep to sneak back to the loft tonight. I didn't stay long the first time, after I let Danny smoothe all the rough edges from running into Gabriel. This time Mom was in bed, the little TV on her dresser flickering softly in the dark. Robin was snoring in her room, one hand on Mr. Purrfect, her orange tiger cat. He blinked at me in the dark when I peeked through the crack in her door, yellow eyes cold and uninterested.

I never know what to tell Danny when he asks questions like that. Your funeral? The fact that Becker still hasn't come back to school because one of his legs doesn't work right, and he's flying on painkillers most of the time anyway? The way Ryan can barely look at me anymore? How much I really hate running into your mom in town, and how often she still looks like she just finished crying?

"Wren?" Anxious, almost pleading. Needy. His

fingers tighten around my arm.

"French," I whisper, letting my lips brush the cool smoothness of his cheek. "Madame Hobart's been on the warpath lately. And I still fuck up pluperfect conjugations."

"I told you, you should've taken Spanish," he says, and he almost sounds like the old Danny when he laughs. "I think Mr. Hill is stoned most of the time."

I can't help but smile at that, because he's right. Mr. Hill wears the same tie for days at a time, and blinks like a startled owl when anyone asks him a question. Danny was always talking about him, back when he was . . . well, still in school.

And still alive, a voice in my head whispers. A nasty, accusing voice, even though I wasn't the reason he died. That was his fault, his and Becker's, for being assholes and taking Becker's car out to the park way on the west edge of town after they'd been drinking. The roads there, a giant spiderweb through the walking trails and trees, are narrow and twisty enough when you're sober and it's daylight.

After I saw a photo of the crash site, Becker's hand-me-down Celica accordioned into the broad base of a chestnut tree, I realized how likely it was that I could have been in the car with them. Give me a beer and I don't make the greatest decisions either.

What was scarier, though, was realizing that, for a minute, I wished I *had* been in the car. That I was gone, too, wherever you go after you die, with Danny.

That's when it started. Knowing that I couldn't turn back time and climb into the backseat the way I had so many other nights, but wanting Danny with me again so much that I started to give serious thought to whether or not I could make that happen.

When I remembered that fluttering white paper bird, I was convinced.

I look at Danny now, just as pale, just as delicate somehow, and he smiles at me. Reaches out to stroke my cheek, tucking hair behind my ear. Snugs his hips closer, all lean, hard bone beneath the jeans I convinced his mom to give me. "He wrote my name on them," I'd told her, pointing to where he'd written it in Sharpie on the inside of one calf, and she'd swallowed tears before she kissed my forehead.

He'd been buried in a dark gray suit and a white shirt with an ice blue tie knotted at his throat. I'd burned it all the day I brought the jeans home. I'd picked up a couple of shirts at the thrift store downtown. The suit smelled like the graveyard, dark and sour, and in it he looked nothing like the Danny I knew.

He brushes his mouth against my hair now, and strokes along my hip, fingers curling in my belt loops, pulling me closer still. I swallow hard, trying not to shudder.

He's so cold now. Always so cold, skin icy smooth. And his body is so quiet—the distant bump of a heartbeat, the thrum of blood flowing through veins, never seemed noticeable until it was gone. I wriggle around to tilt my head up and kiss him, hoping it will be enough.

It never is anymore. For a little while he'll relax, kiss me slowly, lingering and tasting, but it doesn't last.

It's hard to go backward, after all. Even for me, because I can remember what it felt like to let our kisses wander away from our mouths, to peel off clothes to reveal new places to touch, to taste.

I remember the way I could feel his heartbeat in the pulse at his throat, racing and stuttering. How warm he was, his cheeks fevered, his hands hot and firm.

But it's not like that anymore. Not for me, anyway, and every time I have to pull away I'm aware of how strong he is, how much he wants something I can't give him. I can't believe he can't sense the way I tense up, stiff and panicked, or the jackrabbit thump of my own pulse, poised for flight.

Gabriel would. The thought hits me out of nowhere, so unwelcome that I blink and push Danny away too roughly as I struggle to sit up.

Gabriel has no place in my head, and definitely not here in the loft. It's hard not to glance around the dark room, as if, wherever he is, Gabriel can hear what I'm thinking even now.

"Wren," Danny starts, sitting up with me and sliding his arm around my waist. "Don't. Don't . . . stop. You always stop now."

Every word is weighted, heavy with confusion and frustration, and I give in a little and lay my head on his shoulder. It's all my fault, every bit of this. It's like one of those hedge mazes. Once you're in, turned around without any landmarks, there's nothing to do but keep going until you find your way out.

I have a long way to go, I know. Until then, I can only do this: gently push him onto his back, kiss his cheeks, his forehead, his jaw, and whisper, "Sleep now, Danny. Sleep. I want you to sleep."

He can't fight it, even though I can tell he wants to. He doesn't even have to sleep anymore, just as he doesn't need to eat or breathe. But when I tell him something like this, when I give him a direct command, he can't help himself.

I didn't know the spell would work like this, but I'm glad it does. Danny would never hurt me, would never really push himself on me, but there are too many things I can't explain to him now. When he backs me into a corner, this is the easiest way to get around him.

He's frowning, just a little, his brows drawn up in an unhappy question mark, but he doesn't move after a moment. His body relaxes inch by inch, his shoulders softening as they slump against the mattress, his head listing to one side. The hand that had tightened into a fist on his thigh loosens, and I touch the bare, knobby knuckles with one fingertip.

He doesn't stir.

Commands don't last forever. At some point, when I've been away from him too long, I think, he'll wake up.

If I close my eyes, I can see the look on his face in that moment, disappointment and resignation setting his jaw tight. I know because I've seen it when I leave him awake, and it never stops hurting.

This is easier. For me, anyway. This way, I can pretend it's months ago, the first few days after school had ended for the year, and we were curled together in his bed while his mom was at work. It was early summer, the air soft and warm and slightly damp, and he had fallen asleep after . . . well, after.

It was one of the first times I got to watch him sleep, and it was so strange, having him right there but somehow not. The way he sort of melted into the sheets, boneless and completely comfortable, his hair stuck to his forehead in two places, and a thin sheen of sweat on his collarbone. After a while his eyes had started to move beneath his lids as he dreamed, and he suddenly smiled, a startling flare of happiness before his mouth softened again.

That never happens now, no matter how long I watch him. And like everything else, I know that's my fault, too.

CHAPTER SIX

I MANAGE TO AVOID TALKING TO GABRIEL, OR
pretty much anyone, until lunch the next day. I walk
into the cafeteria starved, since I forgot my lunch this
morning, knowing Jess is here somewhere. We only have
lunch and gym together this year.

It smells like sauerkraut and dust and sweat, and I grab
a yogurt and a PB&J from the end of the line. If I eat
quickly, I can probably manage to sneak off to the library
without seeing her, not that I imagine she's looking for
me. When Jess gets her mad on, it usually stays put for a
while.

But it's not Jess I bump into when I turn around, the

pitted plastic tray wobbling in my hands. It's Gabriel, taking a bite of an apple with his head tilted sideways, as if I'm some science experiment he's not sure he executed right.

"God, *what*?" The words are out of my mouth before I can think twice, and he just gives me this amused smile.

"Thought you might want some company," he says with a shrug.

"You thought wrong," I tell him, and head for the tables at the far end of the room. It's the size of the gym, and just as noisy, and the mostly empty table I'm aiming for seems miles away.

Especially since Gabriel follows right behind me, as if I haven't spoken at all, as if I haven't been shooting him "keep away" vibes all day. I think *Stalker* at him, really loud, but when I glance over my shoulder, he only looks sort of confused.

"God, go away," I hiss at him as I set my tray down. The two freshmen at the other end of the table look up, startled, and I roll my eyes. "Not you."

Gabriel pulls out the chair across from mine and sits down, but before I can say anything else, he holds a hand up. "Look, I get it. I shouldn't have . . . I didn't mean to make this weird. But I wanted to say sorry. Okay? It's no big deal. I mean, it is, but . . . I'm not going to say anything."

My heart is pounding again, and I'm so tired of it. It's exhausting, all that adrenaline and whatever it is that makes me the way I am, tingling in my veins like some biological red alert.

I stare at Gabriel for a second, and his cool gray eyes are serious. I know he's not teasing me, even though that would probably be easier to deal with. I flick my gaze to the two girls at the other end of the table. They've stopped eating, mom-made sandwiches still clutched in their hands, and I glare. They grab their paper bags and half-eaten carrot sticks and take off.

"That wasn't nice," Gabriel says, but he's grinning. Slouched across from me in faded navy cords and a plain gray pullover, he actually looks a little too comfortable.

"Freshman girls are the only people I can actually push around, so I have to take advantage sometimes." I fold my arms across my chest and sit back. "What exactly is no big deal? You know, that you're so generously not going to tell everyone."

It's a dangerous move—I don't actually want him to spell it out, especially not here in the cafeteria, but I have to know what he knows.

It's like the first rule of Fight Club. Whatever it is that the women in my family can do, you don't talk about it.

Not even with each other, if my mom's anyone to go by.

I know we're not the only people with something to hide. Everyone keeps secrets—I'm not stupid. No one is, not really. I mean, it only took two weeks in seventh grade for everyone to figure out that when Kayla Schmidt said she was having dinner with her dad once a week, she was really going to a shrink, because she weighed about eighty pounds and sat through every lunch period nibbling a single stalk of celery.

And most everyone knows that Janine French has only slept with three guys, but it's easier to pretend she regularly beds down with the whole football team because that way she's the one being called a slut. Same way it's easier to pretend that no one knows Peter Brannigan's dad hits his mom, because that way there are no awkward conversations, and no reason to feel like you're supposed to be doing something to help.

So yeah, everyone has something to hide, and sometimes it's Very Special Episode stuff and sometimes it's just stupid, like acne all over your back. But as far as I can tell, none of it is going to get you hunted down and burned at the stake.

Okay, that's a little extreme, I know, but I did bring my dead boyfriend back to life. Of a kind, anyway. That's not exactly pulling a rabbit out of a hat.

Gabriel's watching me, and he puts his apple core down on the table before he speaks. "It's not what you're thinking," he says, so low I have to lean forward a little bit. "I can't hear your thoughts, not word for word, not unless I really try, and even then it's not really accurate. You were trying to tell me something before, right? I don't know what it was, but I could feel you sort of . . . poking at me."

Oh. That's . . . unexpected.

I must make a face, because he shrugs. "It's more that sensations sort of come at me? Sometimes images. Like, say someone's across from me on the bus, thinking really hard about her sister. I might get the feeling of worn cotton, or certain colors, or a scent first, and then maybe a memory of them hiding together under the covers, looking at a book, or fighting over the last pancake or whatever, so I know it's her sister and not her mother she's thinking of. See?"

"Sort of." It's like a window, I guess, maybe a distorted one, but still a view right into someone's head. Into someone's heart.

I wonder if he's seen me and Danny, curled up together on my bed before he died, if he can smell Danny's soap, the one he used to use, the way his hands feel on me now, cold and firm.

"It's mostly just plain old clairvoyance," he says, like clairvoyance is just an everyday thing, and I roll my eyes. "I can't see the future, not usually anyway, but I can sometimes see the past. And with most people, what I get, unless I tune it out, is a sort of low-level hum, like feedback. But with you . . ." He stops, tilts his head again, and the weight of his gaze is so heavy, pinning me to my seat. "It's different. Louder, more intense. It's energy, and I know what it means, because my grandmother was like you."

"Like me?" My voice sounds far away, thin and small.

"The power you have." He leans closer, whispering now. "What you can do."

And there it is, cards on the table. I swallow hard, imagining him saying something awful next, something that can't be taken back. Something like *plain old witchcraft*. I don't think of it like that, not even when I do think about people burning me at the stake. It sounds wrong, bad. Dangerous.

And what's more dangerous than bringing the dead to life? the voice in my head whispers, too sweet, like sugar icing on a poison cookie.

"And why did you think I would be happy you could sense that?" I whisper back. My arms are folded so tightly across my chest, the muscles are beginning to twitch, and

I can almost see the flare of panic snapping in the air around me, hot blue fingers pointing the way to run.

"Because I'm different, too." He sounds so urgent, so honest. "How do you think people feel when they realize I know what they're feeling, if not what they're thinking exactly? When I can reach in and find the memory of them wetting their sleeping bag at a sleepover in third grade? Or getting blown off by the guy they like? Or seeing the creepy uncle who touched them the wrong way?"

"But they don't have to know," I hiss at him. "You just don't tell them, and that's the end of it. If anyone catches me . . ." I let the words trail off, hanging there in the sour air of the cafeteria between us, heavy enough to crash.

He doesn't even blink, and his gaze is so steady, so calm, I let it soothe me a little. "I'm not going to say anything, I promise. And we don't . . . I mean, it's not like I'm holding it over your head. It just surprised me. It was cool to find someone else who was sort of like me."

"Freaks of a feather, you mean?" I say, raising an eyebrow, and he rolls his eyes.

"You're really a glass-half-empty person, aren't you?"

"For now I just want to keep my glass to myself," I tell him, but I'm smiling. I can't help it. He looks relieved, like he just stopped short of falling off a cliff.

Or driving his car into a tree, that same voice in my head whispers, and with a bang, it all comes back. Danny's still in Mrs. Petrelli's garage loft, and I'm still the only thing he has in the world.

I haven't even eaten my yogurt or my sandwich, but I push my tray across the table to Gabriel. I'm not hungry anymore.

"Save it for later," he says, and hands me back the sandwich. "Dorsey's class will probably be better with a snack."

I snort, but I stuff it in my bag. The period's almost over anyway, and Gabriel grabs my tray when we stand up. I let him, and I let him walk out of the cafeteria with me, too. It's not a big deal—we're just walking together, not even touching.

Except when we go through the double doors into the hallway, there's Jess, sitting on the window ledge that overlooks the courtyard. David Starger is sitting next to her like the adoring puppy he is when she's around, and Alicia Ferris is venting about something to do with the yearbook—she's the photographer this year, which means that every other page will feature pictures of her.

Jess doesn't look happy. She looks shocked. Even worse, she looks betrayed.

And despite the way my heart sinks, for just a second I feel like telling her to get used to it.

By the time I get to World Lit, all I can think about is damage control. Jess might be a lost cause, but Darcia doesn't deserve to be hurt, not any more than she already has been, anyway. And I know Jess will have told her I was with Gabriel at lunch, when I haven't even been eating with her.

I used to be the one Jess came to when someone had done something outrageous or horrible, like Melissa Schine sleeping with Geoff Dormer before he'd even broken up with Sophie Mathis, or Sketch Harris trashing the music room piano one day when he'd gotten some bad coke.

Jess's sense of justice is pretty bulletproof. For her, there are certain rules everyone is supposed to follow, and they're all unbreakable.

According to Jess's code, I'm pretty sure someone who's still grieving over her dead boyfriend isn't supposed to be walking around school with the new meat, especially when he's as good-looking as Gabriel is. And really especially when she's apparently too depressed to hang out with her best friends.

I slide into my seat next to Darcia, who's already got

her notebook out and a pencil between her teeth as she highlights her notes with a bright pink marker. She gives me a sideways glance and something that wants to be a smile but doesn't quite make it.

"Hey," I say, dropping my backpack on the floor and stretching across the aisle to toe at her leg with one foot. My Doc looks huge and ugly against her faded jeans. "What are you doing after school?"

She blinks twice, and when her mouth opens the pencil falls out, clattering against the desk and into her lap. "Um, what?"

"I am speaking English, right?" I tease her, going for light and joking, the way we've talked to each other forever, until this summer.

But it's too late—her eyes flash confusion at me, like I haven't been her best friend for the last ten years. And it hurts.

"I just thought you might want to come downtown with me, maybe go to the café and hang out for a while," I say, pulling my foot back and sitting up straight. "You wanted to yesterday, so . . ."

It takes her a minute to understand that I'm not kidding, I guess, which hurts even more, and when she smiles, that hurts the most. For a second I wish I could throw my arms around her and tell her I'm sorry, for not being around, for ignoring the fact that she needs me as much as I need her, for everything.

But I can't do that here, so instead I let the sudden bloom of my own relief brighten the dull fluorescent lights and smile back.

CHAPTER SEVEN

SHE'S WAITING BY MY LOCKER WHEN I GET there after last period, earbuds in and her ancient iPod clutched in one hand as she scrolls through the menu. For a minute it all feels so familiar—I can't even count the number of days Darcia or Jess or both of them met me just like this after school, here and in junior high, before we headed off for slices of pizza at Cosimo's or to crash in one of our bedrooms.

But when Darcia looks up at me, I can see the uncertainty in her eyes, and it hurts just as much as it did earlier.

"It's a good day for mochas," I say, fixing my best

normal smile to my face. Maybe if I pretend nothing has changed, she'll start believing it.

"That's true," she says, glancing down the hall at the door. It's gray and windy, and the trees are nearly nude now, shivering as their cast-off leaves swirl along the ground. "I could go for some of Geoff's carrot cake, too."

"No, no, you have to try the pumpkin muffins," I tell her, slamming my locker shut and shouldering my backpack. "He just came up with some new recipe last weekend, and I'm pretty sure they're illegal, they're so good."

She ducks her head when she grins, but she turns off her iPod and pulls out her earbuds as we head outside. Our shoulders bump companionably as we walk, and I hold my breath. This will work, I tell myself. I can do this. I don't have to disappear out of my own life, not completely.

Well, I don't want to. I don't know if that matters very much, but it's true. And as we make our way to Bliss, just like we have so many other afternoons, I ache. It's like a limb I hadn't realized was missing, a really vital one, has suddenly grown back.

The bell over the door jingles when we walk in, and Trevor looks up from his stool behind the counter and grunts a hello. His laptop is open, and he stares at the screen as if it's personally responsible for everything wrong in the world.

If he ever finishes the novel he's apparently been working on since, like, birth, I'm not sure I want to read it.

Darcia takes the table by the window while I wander into the back in search of Geoff. He's taking something out of the oven, and straightens up with streaks of flour like eraser dust on his dark cheeks.

"Hey there, Birdie." He slides the tray onto the nearest counter and leans over to kiss my cheek. "You're not working today."

"Nope. I'm here with Darcia." I poke at one hot muffin and bend down to sniff. Pears, I think, and something else I can't identify, but it smells delicious.

He lifts an eyebrow and dusts off his hands. "Really? You two haven't hung out in forever."

"Spare me the drama." I roll my eyes and snatch a plate of almond cookies off the counter. "Can I make us some mochas or will Trevor have a meltdown?"

"Loverboy's too busy with chapter whatever the hell it is to do much of anything today but glare at decent paying customers. Go for it." He winks when I grin, and I can hear him humming something as I walk out front again.

I set the plate of cookies in front of Darcia, who's

hiding behind her hair and her earbuds from Trevor's suspicious glances. I've told her a million times that he's, well, not nice exactly, just permanently cranky, but she always gives him a pretty wide berth anyway. I'm used to him, since I've been working part-time at Bliss for more than a year, and Geoff has taught me every trick in the book for handling him.

"Mocha?" I ask her, removing one earbud.

She bites into a cookie happily and nods. With her feet tucked up beneath her in the window seat, she looks exactly like the Darcia I've known for so long, and I feel relief bubble up inside me again. The zydeco coming out of the café's speakers swells higher for a second, and Trevor looks up and frowns.

I manage to tamp it down and walk behind the counter to start the mochas. The only other customers in the café are two soccer moms who seem to be coordinating some kind of playdate on their BlackBerrys, and a college kid who's deep into *The Riverside Shakespeare* and keeps mouthing the dialogue as he reads.

It's good. It's right, to be here with Darcia, with Trevor scowling and Geoff baking, and for once I feel like I used to. Normal, or as close to it as I ever get.

But when I sit down, sliding Darcia's mocha across the table toward her, I realize I have no idea what to say.

I don't know what she's been doing since school started, if she's still taking guitar lessons or if she ever talked her mom into letting her get a job. I don't know what new bands she's discovered or what boys she's crushing on, and there are always a few, all admired from afar.

Even when Danny was alive we spent most of our time together. Even when Jess was dating Tyler Ford or that asshole J.D. Springer, and Dar was starting to worry about getting into college. We'd started having weekly sleepovers when we were still young enough to be thrilled that Jess's mom had made Rice Krispies Treats and when staying up past midnight was still a big deal. By the time we were in high school the only difference was that we were talking about how J.D. didn't know that tongue in a girl's ear wasn't a good thing instead of which one of us was going to marry the lead singer of Fall Out Boy one day.

I knew when Darcia got her period, and she knew the day that Jess and I tried smoking. Jess heard all about the time I threw up wine coolers on Will Zorger's shoes, and Dar confided to us that she stole a lipstick from the drugstore downtown. Despite all that history, I suddenly have no idea what to say to her.

I can tell it's not any easier for her. She's put the iPod away again, but she's got her lit notebook open on the table like a shield, and she keeps doodling in the margin instead of looking at me. When she speaks, it's such a surprise I almost spill my drink.

"So you're doing better now?" Her voice is soft, as tentative as always. "About . . . Danny, I mean?"

And there it is. The reason everything is different, even if she doesn't know just how true that is.

"I guess?" I can't help making it a question, because I don't know what else to say. I can't tell her it's really so much worse now.

"I'm sorry." She swallows, looking anywhere but at me, a half-eaten cookie in her hand. "I mean, I'm not saying it's okay now, or that you're okay, that's not what I meant." Her words hang awkwardly in the warm, mocha-scented air. She looks miserable.

"I know what you meant, Dar," I tell her, even though I can feel the sharp edges of all the words I can't say, jagged and painful in my throat. "I'm trying."

That's the truth anyway.

"I know you loved him," she says, and puts down the cookie. It lies like a dusty half-moon on the plate. "How much you loved him. It's not a question of that."

I blink at her. "I never thought it was."

"I know!" She's flushed now, cheeks hot and pink. "I just meant . . ."

"You meant it's a question for Jess because she saw me at lunch with Gabriel." It sounds so stupid out loud. A boy sat with me at lunch and suddenly I'm on trial. God, if either of them knew what was really going on, you could probably hear the screams in Siberia. No, in space.

"Wren." It's only my name, but I can hear questions and explanations and apologies in it. I ignore it, though. I'm too angry to worry about her feelings anymore.

"Don't, okay?" The lights overhead flicker and buzz, but I ignore them, too. "I didn't ask him to sit with me. I didn't ask him to keep talking to me. I don't know what his deal is, okay? It's not like I'm looking for a replacement for Danny, so you can tell Jess to back off."

"Wren." This time it's pained, surprised, almost breathless, and the sound of it is a dart, quick and sharp.

Don't go too far, that voice in my head whispers. *Hold on. You have to hold on to her, to them.*

"I don't mean it like that." I scrub a hand through my hair, and I know it probably looks like demented feathers now, but it doesn't matter. "It's just been a really hard time for me. There aren't rules for this, you know? Do X, Y, and Z and you'll be over it. It doesn't work like that, Dar. And I hate that Jess is judging me for something I haven't even done."

It's a cheap shot and I know it, but it works. Her

expression is startled and defensive when she glances up at me, but I can tell the person she wants to defend is me.

"I can talk to her," she says too fast. "She misses you, too. And we don't know what to do, Wren. How to help. And you seemed to want to be alone, so we did that, but . . . well, we miss you. Jess just gets mad about it."

"I know." And I do. Jess hates to be upset, especially when she feels like she can't do anything about it. And that makes her mad. She's been mad at me a lot the last few months.

"If you could just talk to her . . . ," Darcia begins, and turns those big green-gold eyes on me. She's so hopeful, even when everything looks crappy. I think she was supposed to be a Disney princess instead of a normal kid in a middle-class family.

"I tried that, and she told me to go fuck myself," I say, but there's no heat in the words.

"You didn't try very hard, if she told the story right." She crosses her arms over her chest, and I sit up a little straighter. Darcia doesn't get tough very often, and when she does, she's more pit bull than princess.

And there's that bone-deep hum again, vibrating through me, but this time nothing happens except for the way I open my mouth and speak before I can think twice. It's not magic, it's pure panic.

"Come over next Friday night," I say, and even I can hear the reckless edge to the words. "We'll have a sleepover, just like we used to, all three of us."

Darcia lights up like someone plugged her in, and then it's too late. She blinks at me and swallows hard, and God, if she starts to cry, I'm going to sink into the floor right here, but she holds it together at the last minute.

"I'll help you," she promises, reaching across the table to touch my hand. "I'll talk to Jess first, okay? But you have to call her, too."

"I will." I'm nodding, barely listening as she starts planning. All I can see is Danny, sitting alone on his bed, face twisted into confusion and maybe even panic. Friday nights, or some of them anyway, are his, the one night I can stay in the loft with him if I'm creative with the lies I tell Mom.

Mom, who thinks I've been with Darcia and Jess a dozen or more times since Danny died. That'll be fun, trying to keep them away from her so she doesn't ask any awkward questions about all the other nights I've allegedly been at one of their houses. And then there's Robin, who'll jump all over them like a lonely puppy, looking for the kind of attention they used to give her. All I need is for her to open her mouth about the times she's caught me creeping upstairs late at night when I was supposed to be in bed hours before.

Panic tastes a lot like metal, too bright and cold, and it freezes me in place, one hand curled around my mug and a weak smile on my face as Darcia chatters on about next week.

I figure I should probably get used to the feeling.

Darcia hugs me, one-armed and fierce, on the corner of Elm and Dudley where we always split up to go our own ways home. It's nearly five now, getting darker earlier and earlier every day, and the wind lifts her hair into a tangle of dark brown corkscrews as she walks away. She's facing backward, waving with her free hand, and I can't help smiling.

But the moment I turn around to head up Dudley toward home, my smile falls away. There's Gabriel, hunched into an ancient denim jacket, waiting for me on the next corner.

"Hey," he says when I reach him, and he sounds so easy, so casual, like we're best friends now, that for a second anger prickles just under my skin.

I'm too tired to feed it, though, so I simply nod at him. He falls into step beside me, and suddenly I wonder if he can feel how confused and terrified I am about what I agreed to with Darcia.

"On your way home?" I ask, because distracting him seems like the best option.

"Yeah. I live up on the north end of Prospect."

Not far from me. Naturally. I swallow a sigh. He doesn't seem inclined to say much more, though, so I ask the next thing that comes to mind. "Where'd you go after school?"

"Downtown." He shrugs, and I realize he doesn't even have a backpack. "Looking for a job."

"Oh yeah? Find anything?"

"The guy at the bakery said he'd get back to me, and the manager at the movie theater gave me an application." He gives me a tight smile and turns his head to let the wind blow his hair off his forehead. "It's just me and my sister, so I could use some extra cash."

"Oh." I'm not sure what else to say, and in the thinning light, his eyes are hard to read.

"My mom died a long time ago. My dad isn't around right now."

"Oh. Wow." God, I sound like a complete idiot when I could be telling him I at least know how the second part feels.

"You don't have to be sorry," he says, and he smiles then, a wry and twisted grin that makes me laugh. "I mean, I know it sounds weird, but it's a good thing. My dad being gone, anyway. I miss my mom sometimes, but she was really sick, and she's not now, so . . . I think it's harder for Olivia."

"She's your sister?" We've slowed down, kicking idly at the muddy drifts of leaves on the sidewalk.

"Yeah. She's a bartender at Bar Car, that place down by the train station, and she teaches yoga at the Y some mornings."

I glance sideways at him, but he's focused on the sidewalk, watching as he steps carefully in the middle of each square, avoiding the cracks.

That sounds hard. It's hard enough for us, with just my mom, but at least she's an adult, even if Dad left a cold, empty space behind when he left us. I wonder how old Gabriel's sister is, if she gave up college for this, where their dad is exactly, and suddenly Gabriel turns his head and looks at me with a sly grin.

"Curious, huh?"

I reel back as if he slapped me. "Not fair."

"Well, you're thinking about me, so I figured it was a little bit fair."

"But you couldn't know that unless you peeked." I sound like a little kid about to have a tantrum, and I hate it, but as much as I want to ask him about his grandmother, and what he knows about people with powers like mine, I want to scream, *Don't look!* even more.

Maybe he can feel it anyway, because his grin fades

and he hunches into his coat again as the wind sweeps us farther up the street. "I'm sorry. I was just teasing. Olivia's twenty-four, and no, she never went to college. My dad is, um, another story."

He looks so contrite, almost shy, that I want to apologize, but I won't. I can't, I realize, as I watch his strange eyes darting over at my face, his hair falling forward.

He's just a boy. A cute boy, yeah, a really interesting boy, but just a boy. And I have a boy. I have a *boyfriend*, even if the rest of the world thinks he's gone. I have a boyfriend who has nothing but me, and not even all of me, not anymore. I don't have any business with Gabriel, here and now or any other time. And I can't let him think I do.

So I square my shoulders, hitch my battered JanSport up higher, and set my jaw. "I'm sorry. That sounds rough."

He blinks, surprised by my tone maybe, but before he can say anything I'm pointing at the sign for Edgewood, my street. My stomach twists, sick-hot, because I hate lying, pretending, and it feels like all I do anymore.

"That's me, and I'm late, so I'm going to run. Bye, Gabriel."

My Docs smack the sidewalk as I take off at a run, and if he answers, the wind carries it away.

CHAPTER EIGHT

DANNY SAYS, "YOU DIDN'T MEAN IT," AND PULLS me close. I nod, even though it doesn't really work with my forehead pressed against his chest, and he smoothes a hand down my back. Warm, strong, almost big enough to span it with his fingers outstretched.

Warm. Warm? I turn my head so my cheek rests against his breastbone, and there, just underneath the skin, is the sturdy clock of his heart, ticking steadily.

"Danny . . ."

But when I raise my head to look at him, it's Gabriel, his smile a sudden flash of white. "You didn't mean it," he says, and I nod again, even though I'm not sure what he means.

He smells good, faintly spicy, and he's so warm, so *warm*, I can feel his blood carrying heat through him, pushing up through bone and muscle to skin.

"You didn't mean it," he whispers into my hair, and I close my eyes. I didn't. I know that much. *He* knows that much.

It's his hand stroking my back now, and I'm almost asleep when I hear the thud.

Danny, his eyes like polished stones in the dark, huddled in the corner, his arms around his knees. *Thud.* His head hits the wall with a sickening wet gush. *Thud.*

"You didn't mean it," he says, and Gabriel strokes my back. *Thud.*

"Stop," I whisper, but Gabriel won't let me go. Blood is running down the back of Danny's head, dripping thick and black in the dark onto his shirt. *Thud.*

I open my eyes, panting, as the wall behind my bed shakes. It's Sunday morning, and lately Robin's been practicing headers in her bedroom, so she can bounce the soccer ball off the wall.

I squint at the alarm clock: 10:47. Way too late, even on a Sunday morning, to complain to Mom. I bury my head under the pillow instead, but it doesn't help. I can feel the vibrations.

I can see Danny's face. *Thud.*

I bang on the wall with one balled-up fist and sit up to throw back the covers. I hate Sundays.

Sundays are the only days the salon is closed, so they used to be awesome. Sundays meant pancakes or waffles for breakfast and lingering around the table with the radio on. Sundays were when Mom cut our hair right there in the kitchen, or we convinced her to curl or braid it or put it up in elaborate knots. When we walked to the playground or went to the mall, when we made cookies on rainy afternoons or went to the matinee at the dollar theater on the south side of town. Dad's been gone so long that Robin doesn't remember other weekends, when the four of us went to the park or downtown for pizza, or curled up on the sofa in one big pile on winter days, watching a movie.

I remember, but Dad's been gone so long that the ache of missing him is dull, a vague sore spot that I know not to touch. It's harder not to poke at the memories of Aunt Mari and Gram.

It's different now, anyway. We're older, for one— even Robin isn't into sitting around playing hairdresser anymore. She has soccer practice on Sundays in the fall and the spring, and I sometimes have shifts at Bliss. Mom uses the day to do laundry and clean the bathroom, which she doesn't trust either of us to do right, and usually spends the afternoon sprawled on the sofa with a DVD or a book.

Even last spring, I might have joined her, curled up to watch a cheesy movie or let her quiz me on my French vocabulary. Before Danny died, in other words. Before I had so much to hide.

Now it's the hardest day to get out back to see Danny—even if Mom decides to hit the supermarket, she's never gone for more than an hour or two, and when we're both home, I can feel the weight of her gaze on me like a physical thing.

She's in the kitchen when I go downstairs, and she looks up from folding clean laundry on the kitchen table when I head for the coffeemaker.

"She's doing it again." I close my eyes as I lift my mug to my nose and breathe deep. If I can concentrate, the dream will fade out, disappear like the steam curling out of my mug.

"I need a little more information than that, babe." I can hear the smile in her voice. It's a good day, then. I know she's been busy at the salon, and that always makes her happy.

"Robin. Soccer ball. Wall." I slouch into the chair across from her and set my mug down.

"Hey, don't splash," Mom says, and then cocks her

head, listening. Upstairs, there's a distant *thud*, *thud*, *thud*, and she sighs. "Well, it got you out of bed. I'm not sure I can complain."

"It's *Sunday.*"

"Not working today?" Above the T-shirt of Robin's she's folding, her eyes are calm and simply curious, the same gold-flecked green as Robin's. Mine are plain brown, the color of dried mud.

"I worked yesterday," I tell her, and breathe in the caffeine-rich steam of my coffee again. Mom's always up and out early on Saturdays, since that's the salon's busiest day. Robin usually has a game, and then spends the afternoon with Mom doing homework and answering the phone at the front desk.

"Do you have homework to do today?"

"Always," I groan, and pick through the laundry when I spot my favorite shirt. "But I'm going to see Becker later."

Mom makes a noncommittal *hmm* noise, but I can feel her watching me as I finish my coffee and set the mug in the sink. I hate that she doesn't trust me anymore, but I hate more that I know she shouldn't. Half of what I tell her is a lie, and I never meet her eyes these days if I can help it.

Even now, I'm wondering if I can get down Clark and over to Rosewood and to the loft before I come home.

I've never left Danny alone for a whole day, and he was strange last night, his fingers too tight where they were twined with mine as I said good-bye.

Thud. I can still hear it, still see his face, smooth as stone, empty, his eyes flat and unseeing. I turn around and paw blindly across the counter for the basket of fruit, anything to focus on.

Robin bangs into the kitchen as I'm peeling a banana, soccer ball balanced in one hand and her practice bag slung over her shoulder.

"Ooh, look, she's risen from the dead," she says, and I nearly choke on my banana.

"No thanks to you," I manage a moment later, when Mom frowns. "Soccer is an *outdoor* sport, genius."

"Whatever." She's got the attitude down already, I have to give her that, even if she is still twelve. "I'm the only girl on the team who can head the ball, and I have to practice."

I roll my eyes at her this time, even though it is sort of cool—I've been to a couple of her games, and she's really good, a sturdy little streak of lightning on the field, her feet always moving. She loves sports the way I, well, don't, and it's pretty awesome.

I don't tell her that, though. Her head is big enough as it is.

She's rooting around in the fridge for something when Mom says, "Do you want a ride over to Becker's?"

I wonder if she knows how long it takes me to get there when I walk. Not because it's far, but because I drag it out. Ryan and I trade off visiting Becker, but I hate it. "Nah, I'm good."

"If you're sure." She stands up and puts the last folded T-shirt on the top of the pile, and for a minute I want to bury my head on her shoulder, tell her I'm not sure, that I don't want to go at all, that I need her to fix everything for me. But the time when I could have done that is long past.

Instead, I let her ruffle my hair as she walks past me. "I think I'll swing by and get Robin after practice, maybe head to the mall. You guys could use a couple of winter things, I bet. And we can get some lunch, too, Binny."

"Really?" Robin is beaming. She turns to set her water down on the counter and her grip on the soccer ball slips—for just a second, when she catches sight of it, it hangs there in midair like a wobbly little planet, and I can feel the air tighten, thick and heavy the way it feels before a thunderstorm.

She blinks, surprised, and catches it before it hits the floor, and both of us look at Mom.

Her lips are pressed tight together, but she doesn't

freak. Instead, she just says, "You'll be done by one, right? I'll pick you up."

Robin lets out a relieved breath and heads for the front door, calling over her shoulder, "See you!"

And then it's just me and Mom again. I glance out the window at the backyard, where the roof of the loft is just visible through the trees, and my stomach swoops low and fast as I picture the Danny in my dream.

Between going to see Becker and checking on Danny, it's hard to say which I want to do less.

Becker's mom answers the door when I ring the bell a few hours later. She always looks vaguely guilty to see me, pale eyes flicking everywhere but at my face. Becker was driving the car, after all.

"George is upstairs." She stands back to let me pass, and I can smell something on the stove in the kitchen, dark and spicy. Mrs. Becker used to work downtown at the health clinic, but she quit after the accident to take care of Becker. He's the youngest, "her baby," she told me the day I went to see him in the hospital, and now whenever I go to the house something is cooking.

I don't know where all the food goes, because both she and Becker look like they haven't eaten in months.

There's a distant grunt when I knock on Becker's

door, just audible over the sound of the TV. I push the door open and squint. The shades are drawn and the room is nearly night-dark aside from the light of the big flat-screen TV mounted to the wall opposite the bed.

Becker glances at me, and I can tell he's high. He's still on painkillers, even though I heard the doctors wanted him to stop. And I know that K.J. Simon sneaks him pot when he comes over. I can't believe his parents can't smell it—he doesn't even bother to wheel himself toward the window when he smokes, and the grassy, burnt scent of weed is baked into the curtains and the comforter now.

"Hey, Wren." He's sprawled on the bed, his mangled leg still braced and awkward. I take a couple of magazines off the easy chair in the corner and sit down as he struggles up on his elbows, wrenching himself into a sitting position.

"What're you watching?"

"Nothing." He picks up the remote and clicks the TV off, and I try not to cringe. It's easier when he leaves it on, when we can spend an hour silently watching a stupid movie or guys on BMX bikes coming this close to breaking their necks.

I was never really angry at him, although everyone assumed I would be. That's what his mom thinks, I know, and what Becker thinks, too. He can't look at me, either, unless he's really wasted, and then he can't stop talking, apologizing and crying and holding my hand.

I hate those days.

I should be furious with him. He bought the beer; he drove the car; he was speeding, laughing, not paying attention, drunk and goofing around like nothing in the world could hurt either him or Danny. But when I look at him now there's nothing but a whistling emptiness in my chest.

Becker's always been the clown, and he could afford to be. He's that kind of athletic good-looking, not as tall as Danny, and a little broader, but still pretty graceful. His parents have money, the kind that gets you into good schools even when you don't have the best grades. He was always the one grabbing Danny and Ryan to cut afternoon classes and go drink beer up in the woods, or sneak into a movie.

Now no one can say if he'll ever walk again, at least without a crutch and a definite limp, even if he does get his act together and concentrate on physical therapy.

He rubs his eyes and takes a deep breath like he's working up to saying something, and I wish he wouldn't. Mostly I just wish I could leave, but Becker's my friend, too, and sometimes I feel bad, because I think I should feel worse. Becker lived through the accident, but life as he knows it is over.

"How are you?" he says, the words slurring together a little bit.

I shrug. "I should be asking you that."

He makes a dismissive noise and shakes his head. "The same, pretty much."

"Me too, I guess."

His face twists a little, and he doesn't look at me when he says, "I'm so sorry, Wren. I just wish . . ."

"Becker, don't." I can't listen to it today. "Let's watch something, okay?"

He doesn't answer me for a minute, and doesn't look up from the rumpled mess of his blue plaid comforter, and I wonder if he's fallen asleep, or if he's just really high. But in a moment he lifts his head, and his eyes are glassy, bright.

I turn to face the TV as he clicks it on, and we watch some behind-the-scenes thing on a metal band I've never heard of. I don't care, though. It's better than talking.

And it's a lot better than thinking about how neither one of us can let go, Becker of the boy he was before the accident, and me of the boy I lost. Holding on isn't doing either of us any good, but it's too late to change it now, for me anyway.

He's asleep when I look at him later, head drooping

onto one shoulder, the skin under his eyes smudged dark and too thin. I turn off the TV when I leave, and I don't wonder what he dreams.

I stop at Bliss for a coffee on the way home, and I'm walking up Elm when Mom pulls up at the curb and honks. "Jump in," she calls. She's grinning, like this is the happiest accident ever, and I can't think of a good excuse to refuse even with Danny still alone in the loft.

We stop at the supermarket on the way home, and Robin proposes that we make enchiladas together, which we haven't done in ages. She's all lit up, flushed and bubbling over in ways I'm not sure she even notices— the fire Mom sets in the fireplace flickering higher when Robin sits down in front of it, the dented bell peppers firming up, glossy again, when she takes them out of the grocery bag. She came home with three new shirts and a pair of earrings, and it's sweet, how happy an afternoon at the mall with Mom makes her.

We're just sitting down to eat when my phone buzzes in my jacket pocket. Mom lifts an eyebrow but doesn't protest, even though cell phones are forbidden at the table when we're sitting down to a meal all together. We're having a good evening, and it makes me realize how long it's been since we've done this kind of thing.

I pull out my phone and glance at the screen: Jess. Great.

We talked after school on Friday, if you can call it that. It felt like some sort of bizarre peace negotiation, both of us mumbling we were sorry without really looking at each other, and Darcia standing in as referee, prodding us to discuss my plan for a sleepover. But I could tell Jess saw how happy Dar was, and since I'd been careful to steer clear of Gabriel all day, she didn't have anything to call me on.

Of course, after the way I'd blown Gabriel off Thursday afternoon, he barely looked at me in class anyway, much less came to find me at lunch. It stung, like the shock of cold water in your lungs.

"Hey," I say when I answer my phone now, trying to sound as normal as possible. As far as Mom knows, Jess and I spend as much time together as ever, even if it's not at our house.

"Hey," Jess says back, and there's silence for a minute, a weird stalemate. She said she'd be busy most of Saturday, but that she'd call today. Now she has, and without Darcia here to mediate, I'm not sure what to say. Clearly, neither is Jess.

But Mom is looking at me as she bites into a piece of pepper, and I scramble.

"We're eating dinner."

There's another brief silence before Jess says slowly, "Okay. Um. So what's the deal with Friday?"

I can picture her in her room, on the bed on her back, knees bent as she stares at the ceiling. It's a big room, bigger than either Dar's or mine, but it's a bigger house, too. Jess's mom works in the art department of an advertising agency, and her dad is a lawyer on Wall Street, and Jess and her older brother, Matt, are the only kids.

They're like a TV family, except without the funny next-door neighbor or the weird uncle, and they're so normal and nice to one another, it's almost boring. Every once in a while, I wonder if one day we'll find out her dad is really an ax murderer or her mom snorts coke and has affairs with the pool guy. They actually have a pool, so that part makes a sort of sense.

It makes me wonder what my life would be like if Dad hadn't left. If he and Mom would still be as stupid in love as they were when I was a kid, the way Jess's parents are. If anything would have changed—my power, dating Danny—because he was still around.

"Um, what about it?" I say, hoping she didn't hear the demented squeak in my voice.

Jess sighs. "Like . . . God, I don't know, Wren. We haven't seen you in forever, and now we're having some shiny happy sleepover like everything's cool? It's random."

She's right, it's bizarre, and it's all my fault that it is, but it still twists my heart into a hard little knot to hear her say it.

And what am I supposed to say, here at the dinner table with Robin sitting next to me, chattering to Mom about some werewolf movie she wants to see, and Mom glancing at me every couple of seconds, her chin propped on her fist?

"Look, if you don't want to come over," I say, turning sideways a little bit and lowering my voice, "just say so. I mean, I thought . . . I don't know what I thought."

Jess sighs again, a gust of weariness.

"No, I want to. I just hate that we're . . . I don't know. Are we fighting? I don't even know anymore."

"We're not fighting." I know Mom can hear me, even though I'm speaking as softly as I can. "We don't have to, anyway."

"Did you ask your mom about Friday yet? Is it okay?"

It used to be okay all the time. Mom's always happy for Jess and Dar to come over—she never minds if I'm at one of their houses, but she loves it when I have friends here. To keep an eye on me? Maybe. Sometimes I think she just likes the noise, the extra life in the house.

"No, but I will. You know she won't care," I say, and grunt when Robin elbows me in the ribs as she bends down to get something she dropped.

"Okay." She doesn't sound entirely convinced, and now Mom is frowning at me. Robin gets up to clear her plate, so it's time to wrap this up.

"I'll call you later," I tell Jess. "I have to go."

"Well, I'll be here, wrestling Finch's trig problems into submission. If I don't answer, assume I'm comatose."

She sounds a little more like herself then, and I grin as I say good-bye. Maybe this will work. Maybe I'm panicking for nothing.

Then I catch sight of Mom's suspicious expression. Maybe not.

"Who was that?" she asks as I dig into my enchilada again, and she runs a finger around the rim of her mug.

"Just Jess."

"And what won't I care about?" She tilts her head, waiting, and I take the plunge.

"Jess and Darcia sleeping over on Friday night."

Robin's clattering something in the sink, and in the living room the fire is still crackling and the TV is on, but for a second it's completely silent, just the two of us, eyes locked. She knows something is up, she's known for months, but she doesn't know what, and this is just part of it. No matter what I've told her about hanging out with Darcia or going downtown with Jess, they haven't been at the house since shortly after Danny died.

Like I said, she's not stupid.

Still, she simply blinks as she says, "Of course. They're more than welcome, you know that."

My heart thumps back into rhythm then, and Robin says, "Mom, you got ice cream! Awesome."

I snort, and Mom smiles and gets up. She leans down to press her head to mine as she clears her plate. I lean into the clean, warm-cotton scent of her, and pretend that it's all going to be just that easy.

CHAPTER NINE

IT'S NEARLY MIDNIGHT BEFORE I CAN GET OUT to the loft. Where was I going to say I was going at eight on a Sunday night, once dinner was cleaned up and we'd stuffed ourselves with mint chocolate chip and butter pecan? Nowhere, of course. So I pulled out my chemistry book and studied while Robin watched some ridiculous movie and Mom went over the schedules for the salon.

The cat darts between my legs now when I open the back door, and I hiss at him to come back. He pauses mid-sprint and looks at me, tail twitching, and then takes off again. I sigh and follow him, taking care not to let the screen door slam.

It's freezing out, and I hunch into my hoodie as I run across the backyard. Everything sounds too loud in the dead calm of the hour, and I wince every time my foot snaps a twig. The side door to the garage wheezes on its ancient hinges when I open it, and I swallow hard. Mrs. Petrelli is asleep in the house, and even if she isn't, she has to be way too deaf at her age to hear it.

Danny isn't, though. He grabs me when I clear the top step, and muffles my startled scream with one hand. He's no warmer than it is outside, and the smooth skin of his palm is too earthy, dark.

Dead.

I wrestle out of his grasp when I can breathe again, and he stumbles back toward the bed.

"Wren, Wren, where were you? *Wren.*"

If I close my eyes, I can see him banging his head against the wall, smell the hot copper of the blood.

"I'm here," I tell him, and sit down abruptly on one of the wooden crates. "I'm right here, it's okay."

"Wren." He practically vaults forward, landing on his knees in front of me, and lays his head in my lap. "You weren't here. You weren't here for so long."

I touch his head, spreading my fingers in his hair. It's so dry, so cool, dark straw now. "I'm sorry," I whisper, and my voice shakes as I make myself stroke his head. "I couldn't help it."

"I need you here, Wren." He shrugs away from my hand and lifts his head to look at me. His fingers dig into my thighs, ten distinct points of pressure. "I *need* you. When you're not here, I don't . . . I can't think. I don't know what to do and I can't . . . I can't *think*, Wren."

The hair on the back of my neck prickles, and I shut my eyes again. I can't look at his face, his mouth twisted and his brow knotted, his cheeks pale, and so, so cold.

"I didn't mean to," I whisper, and try not to flinch when his palm rests against my face, his thumb lightly tracing my cheekbone. "I didn't mean to."

I tell him stories for a while, lying on the mattress with him, his head cradled on my chest. I've pulled up the blankets, but it doesn't matter. The chill is on him, in him, and he's pressed up against me. My teeth are chattering, but if he notices, he doesn't say anything.

He loves this, but I have to be careful. I try to talk only about us, times when we were alone together, because I don't want to remind him of Ryan or Becker, or his parents and his brother and sister. I can't answer the questions he asks about them, not honestly anyway.

He never used to ask. At first, all he wanted was me, as if he'd woken up in some dream where the two of us were all there was, all he needed. Even the loft didn't confuse him much, as long as I was there.

But the longer he's alone, the more the dream fades.

"Remember the first time we went into the city?"

He nods, calmer now, and his hand rests easy on my hip. We've been at this for an hour, and I dread the thought of my alarm in the morning.

"God, it was so cold that day, even for February," I whisper, and shiver a little. It doesn't feel much warmer right now.

I describe it all for him, letting my eyes drift shut as I lay my head back and remember it. Bundled together into the seat, sharing earbuds and a coffee while the train rattled along the tracks. Changing at Newark and running down the long ramp to the PATH, which took us into the Village. We'd stopped every two blocks for coffee, it seemed—it was a blue-cold day, the wind biting into our cheeks, and we didn't have anything specific to do anyway. We were simply roaming, playing, and it became a game to spot another coffee shop first and race toward it on the crowded streets.

"My favorite was that one on MacDougal," I say with a smile. "The one with the tin ceiling and all those old pictures of people in furs and weird hats. That place had the best croissants."

He makes a vague humming noise, in agreement, I think, and I know he won't fall asleep, but he's as relaxed as he ever gets now.

"And then we went to Bleecker Bob's and that comic-book store, remember? Oh, and the thrift store where you bought me that necklace, the one with the owl in front of the moon."

"I remember the moon." He sounds faraway, preoccupied, and his body is tense again, solid marble.

"Yeah, the owl is sitting on a branch with the full moon behind it," I tell him, and scritch idly through the hair at his nape. "It's pretty. I'll wear it tomorrow."

"I remember the moon," he says again, and sits up. The blankets rustle in his wake, and I shiver. "And the candles. There were candles."

My stomach turns over in a dizzying swoop. Candles? There are no candles on that necklace, but there were candles and a full moon the night I cast the spell.

I grab his arm, trying to pull him back to me. The silver light through the window is murky, but his eyes are gleaming.

Polished stones, I think, remembering my dream, and pull harder.

"Remember where we went after that?" I ask him. I'm trying not to panic—he's immovable, completely still, watching me, and I feel small, weak.

Breakable.

Danny never had much of a temper, but this isn't really Danny in too many ways to count. I know that my Danny would never have hurt me, would have stepped in front of a bus before hitting me, but this Danny? I'm suddenly not sure. As cold as he is, I can feel the heat of fury in his stare.

"Remember?" I say again, and my voice is really shaking now, giving the word at least four extra syllables. Panic is fluttering like a trapped bird in my chest, and the air snaps with electricity. "We found that great diner on Broadway and you ordered the cheeseburger that was as big as your head."

I don't even know what I'm saying anymore, but I let the words keep coming, the cherry cheesecake we shared, the long, windy walk back to the PATH station, the woman with the blind Great Dane and the feathered hat, the ridiculous T-shirt Danny bought from the vendor in the train station.

After a minute, he softens, and his eyes fall shut, maybe picturing the scenes I'm describing. I pull him toward me again, gently, slowly, and he comes, stretches out beside me to bury his nose in my hair.

"I remember," he says, and I can only hope he means that stupid vampire shirt.

★ ★ ★

Gabriel throws a pen at me in trig, and I jerk out of a doze before Ms. Nardini notices. I scrawl "thank you" on my notebook, but he doesn't smile, just nods.

I can't worry about him or his hurt feelings—I'm barely functional, even with two cups of coffee before school. It was close to two thirty before I snuck back into the house last night, and the four hours of sleep I got feels more like four minutes.

Anyway, looking at him is no easier than being with Danny. Every time I spot him out of the corner of my eye, I can hear his voice in my ear, feel his hand on my back, smell the musky boy scent of his shirt against my cheek.

But that was just a dream. What happened with Danny last night was real, and that's what frightens me.

I drag myself through my morning classes and stumble into the cafeteria at lunchtime, desperate for more caffeine and a chance to put my head down and pass out, but Jess is waiting when I walk through the doors.

"Sit with me?" she says simply, and I can only nod. I can't screw this up on top of everything else, and even if I can't tell her anything about what's going on, I find myself hoping that we can hang out like we used to. Laughing at things only we understand, finishing each other's sentences, passing each other the parts of our lunch that we don't want but the other might.

She takes a table by the windows while I get a soda and a hot dog with Tater Tots. It looks disgusting, but it's better than the nothing I packed, and at least it'll give me something to do with my hands.

Jess has a salad from the gourmet deli downtown, and she hands me a pile of mushrooms and green peppers as soon as I sit down. I grin and toss a Tater Tot into her greens, and she smirks. It feels good, almost like normal, until I realize, just like with Darcia, I have no idea what to say. I don't know what Jess is up to lately outside of trig problems, and that's a pretty lame subject to get into.

But as soon as she swallows her Tater Tot, she launches into a story about how Ian Sparks left a note in Diane Cashdollar's locker this morning, complete with earnest declarations of love and, apparently, hand-drawn hearts.

The funniest thing about this is that Ian is gorgeous and six foot two, but because he's a freshman, he's completely off Diane's radar. She's a senior, and she takes gorgeous to a whole other level. If she had any sense, she'd ditch Mark Collins, who cheats on her during every away football game, especially since Ian is sweet, and will probably treat her like the princess she desperately wants to be.

She doesn't have any sense, though, so that's that. And

I hate to sympathize with Ian, since I think he's more boob-struck than love-struck, anyway.

Gossip takes us safely through the lunch period, and when we walk out, Jess seems as much like her old self as I could have hoped. She even elbows me, teasing and grinning, when we separate in the west hall to go our own ways. It makes World Lit easy, since I can tell Darcia that we ate lunch together, but none of it erases the low hum of worry just under the surface.

It's all stirred up inside me, this bubbling happiness that maybe I didn't completely screw up my friendship with Jess and Darcia, and a hot, twisting sickness in my gut at the thought of what Danny might say or do when I climb up to the loft. The mess of it is making me dizzy, and when I walk home I drag the wind along with me, a chilly swirl that blows up my jacket and settles on the back of my neck.

I'm taking the long way home, too, which is stupid. If anything, the longer I take to get there, the more frantic Danny will be.

This end of Dudley is busy with North Avenue so close, a rush of cars zipping in either direction, and I have no warning when a hand closes over my shoulder. I'm so startled, I nearly trip over my own feet, but Gabriel grabs my arm and pulls me upright.

"Sorry," he says, and he looks so stricken I can't be mad.

"It's okay. I was . . . somewhere else." I huddle into my coat as we stand there on the corner of Dudley and Forest, even though I know I'm the reason for the cold fingers of air pushing through Gabriel's hair.

"Hey, I just wanted to tell you . . ." He tilts his head to one side, steps a little closer. "I asked around about you. I know you probably didn't want me to, but I know about Danny."

I can't help it—I hear the words and I blow wide open, a door banging in the wind.

I see my mistake as soon as I make it—Gabriel meant he heard about Danny dying, probably figured it explained why I run so hot and cold, and wanted nothing more than to offer sympathy. Instead, his mouth hangs open as he stares, and I wonder what he's seeing. The graveyard in the moonlight, candles flickering in a closed circle? The loft with its ratty nest of a bed and the boy waiting on it, pale and still?

"*Wren.*" Gabriel grabs my arm again, harder this time, pulling me off the corner and up Forest, behind the screen of a giant maple, its nude branches creaking overhead like bones. "Wren, what did you do?"

CHAPTER TEN

IT'S TOO MUCH—THAT HUMMING ENERGY surges inside me and a branch snaps above us, clattering to the ground only two feet away. Gabriel's fingers dig into my upper arm, and he steers me back toward Dudley. I'm breathless, trying to keep up, when I manage to get out, "Wait, stop, my house is that way."

"Later," he says, grim and determined, and we cover two blocks in a blur, leaves crunching underfoot as we head toward Prospect. Five minutes later we're climbing the stairs inside a rambling old house and he's shoving a key into the door on the second floor.

"Sit," he says tersely, and I bristle.

"What are you, my father?" It's stupid, and hardly the point, but I don't care. I'm horrified and panicked and exhausted, and that's just on the surface. Beneath all of that it's even darker, smoky and dirty and wrong and regretful, and I close my eyes as I drop onto the sagging sofa.

Gabriel ignores me and goes into the kitchen through the arch to the right, and I hear the tap running, the distant *snick* as a burner is lit. I'm trembling, blood racing so fast through my veins I can practically feel the hot course of it snaking in and out of my heart. I drag my feet onto the sofa and wrap my arms around my legs, willing myself to calm down.

This is bad. I know there are words worse than *bad*, but I can't even think of them. I was stupid to let Gabriel get close, and now who knows what could happen?

I startle when wood scrapes against the bare floor and open my eyes to find Gabriel sitting on the coffee table in front of me. He hands me a glass of water.

"Here. Until the tea's ready."

I take it, sloshing some over the edge since my hand is still shaking. It's cool and wet and just what I didn't know I needed, and when I'm done, I hand the glass back to Gabriel.

His eyes are dark gray now, the color of a coming

storm, and I swallow hard. He's seen things about me no one has seen, not even Mom, and it's frightening. I don't want to lie all the time, but I don't want to be judged, either.

I do enough of that for everybody.

"Does anyone know?" he says, setting the glass on the table next to him.

I snort. "Are you high? Who would believe it?"

He doesn't even flinch, and I bite my lip. The snark comes naturally, but he doesn't deserve it.

"Tell me." He leans forward, resting his arms on his knees, and he's so close I catch the scent from my dream, cotton and boy sweat and something else, too, sharp and bright.

It's instinct again that makes me delay the inevitable. "Tell you what?"

"All of it. I mean, I could tell you had power, but this is . . ." He shakes his head. "Tell me."

I wish I could just let him *see* instead. It's suddenly so shameful, my grief, my need, my selfish, ridiculous belief that I could have what no one else gets to have without consequences.

I can't believe I was actually stupid enough to think I could bring my boyfriend back from the *dead* and walk off into some movie happy ending.

I am the kid who sticks her finger in the light socket. I am the person who doesn't check the expiration date on the milk. I am the idiot who has never looked before she leaped. I am the girl who is falling apart, right now.

"Tell me," he repeats, and circles his fingers around the stalk of my ankle.

Instead of intimidating me, it grounds me, connecting us, and I raise my gaze to his face again.

"What did you hear about how he died?"

"Does it matter?"

It doesn't, I guess. Death is death, and if Danny had died of some horrible, lingering disease, I can't imagine I would have mourned differently, or less.

What matters is how much I loved him. How well I loved him. That's where it all started, right or wrong.

I want to tell Gabriel that, explain that much, at least—I didn't do what I did on a whim. I didn't take it lightly, even if I didn't really understand what it would mean.

Before I can say anything, though, he squeezes gently, and nods. "I know. I can . . . I know that part. Tell me the rest."

Bringing Danny back was nothing like what I had imagined.

I wasn't exactly functional those first few days after Ryan called with the news. I remember snatches—the smoking hole in my floor, my mother's hand on my head, steady and soft, Jess and Darcia hovering in the door to my room, their faces blurred through my tears and sheer exhaustion. Until the funeral, I didn't move far off my bed, curled up under the covers, even in the July heat, holding on to a green and blue wool scarf of Danny's because it smelled like him.

It wasn't until two days after the funeral, when I saw the pictures of the crash, that I thought of the fragile white paper bird I had created.

I spent the next week on the internet, holed up in my room with the groaning laptop I shared with Mom and Robin. By the end of the third day, my eyes were burned dry and my head hurt from staring at the screen too long, but I had a few ideas about where I could look for spells. Just the thought of it made a nervous thrill ripple beneath my skin—whatever it was that I could do, it had always just happened before. The most I had ever done was concentrate on what I wanted, like the rain in Robin's room. A spell seemed so foreign, strangely official. But I was pretty sure I couldn't just wish Danny back to life.

Once last year, before I met Danny, I had asked Aunt Mari about whether she'd ever looked into incantations or lore about the craft. We were shopping at the thrift store on the south side, picking through old clothes and vintage stuff for her Halloween costume, and she looked up at me over a rack of circa-1980s dresses and frowned.

"I don't think of it that way," she said, and narrowed her eyes as she thought about it. "I know other people do, even people who can do what we do, I guess. But it's more natural than that to me, and that's part of the gift. Figuring out what you can do, using your skill organically, the same way you would if you figured out you were a good cook. Then you might add ingredients to things or create your own recipes."

It sounded a little woo-woo even to me, and I was thankful she'd lowered her voice. But she was serious, and I knew it. When I thought back, I couldn't remember her or Mom ever reading a book of spells, and certainly not brewing up some potion on the stove. What I remembered was how spontaneous it always seemed, spur-of-the-moment magic that just sort of happened.

She grabbed a long black dress off the rack and sucked her cheeks in as she held it up to her chest. "Morticia Addams is probably too much for the preschool Halloween parade, huh?"

And that was that. I didn't push, not then, and after Danny was dead I definitely didn't want anyone to suspect what I was thinking about, so I just started poking around the web and the library, looking up anything I could find on the occult.

The occult. Even the thought that what I was doing qualified as the occult seemed wrong somehow, not that it stopped me. I hopped a train into the city one Saturday morning, and it was sort of frightening, how easy some of the stuff was to find, once I knew where to look. Maybe no one without the power I had could work a spell, but maybe they could. And there were road maps all over the place, it turned out, for anyone who wanted to make the trip.

I found the book I needed in a little store way down on the Lower East Side. It was tiny, down a short flight of steps in the basement of an old row house, and the whole place wore its coat of dust as if it just couldn't be bothered to take it off anymore. Half of the shelves were empty, and the signs behind the register were all badly hand-lettered on ancient, yellowing pieces of notebook paper.

I don't know what I was expecting, but the guy behind the counter looked like my seventh-grade science teacher. His hair was combed over sideways to hide a bald spot, and he had on a stained white button-down and khakis that looked like the grime was the only thing holding them together.

"We do a lot of business on the web," he said when he caught me looking around. "Special orders."

"I'm thrilled for you," I said, and started through the books lining one shelf. A lot of them looked like they were Wicca Lite, but there was a good handful of older books, too, well-thumbed volumes with cracked leather or cloth bindings. I picked three and carried them up to the counter, where Creepy Guy raised a thick black eyebrow.

"Pretty heavy reading there, kid."

"I'm in Mensa," I said, getting out my wallet.

"Smart doesn't have anything to do with this stuff."

"Cool. Then maybe you'll want to borrow them when I'm done." I gave him a sweet smile and waited. "You going to give me a price or what?"

He shook his head, but he toted up *The Burnside Grimoire*, *The Compendium of Shadow Magick*, and a book by Aleister Crowley. I'd read on the internet that he was some famous occult guy from the turn of the century who was into all kinds of what he called "magick." I was lucky I had my ticket home—I was out nearly a hundred dollars, all the money I had saved at the moment.

"Good luck," Creepy Guy called as I left, the brown paper bag of books stuffed into my backpack. I closed my eyes and focused, and just as the door shut behind me, a cloud of slate-colored smoke mushroomed into the shop, tickling the back of my legs.

It was just smoke, not fire, and it was petty and wrong, but I didn't care. I paid for a soda from a cart on the corner when I knew I had enough money left for the subway, and spent the ride home sneezing, my nose buried in the musty books.

It should have gotten scarier the more I researched. When you find yourself buying mandrake root on the internet, it's probably a good time to question what you're doing.

But the more I read, page after page of incantations and phases of the moon and streams of energy, the better I could see Danny's face again. Not the waxy, blank one I had seen in his casket. *Danny*, laughing, shaking the hair off his forehead, rolling his eyes at Becker's weak Borat impression, leaning in to kiss me, his wide, soft mouth curved up on one side.

I wanted him back. I wanted him back so much I couldn't think about anything else. Everywhere I looked was suddenly somewhere Danny wasn't. My hands were empty because Danny wasn't holding them. My room echoed with quiet because Danny wasn't there whispering ridiculous things to make me laugh, or make me shiver.

It seemed so right. Danny was mine, I was his, and that

wasn't going to work if he was dead. So I would make him not dead, not anymore. I didn't think any further than what it would feel like to kiss him again, to wrap my arms around him and bury my head against his shoulder.

That was my first mistake. It also turned out to be the biggest.

Gabriel pushes a hand through his hair, mouth set in a tight line. "Then what?"

I finished the strong tea he brought halfway through my story, and now my throat is dry. "I had to wait for the right time."

"Full moon?"

I nod, hating the look in his eyes. Pity, horror, something a little like awe, but not the good kind. The kind that "awful" comes from.

"Tell me," he says for probably the thirtieth time. "The details, Wren."

"Why does it matter?" I huff out a breath and sink back against the sofa. "You know how it turned out."

"It matters, Wren." The sharp edge of his voice slices through the room. "It matters because it determines what you brought back."

"What are you talking about? I brought back *Danny*."

"Come on, Wren." For the first time in over an hour,

he gets up, and the coffee table screeches against the floor as he pushes off it. He rakes his fingers through his hair again as he paces toward the windows. "Is he really the Danny you knew?"

The cold knot in my stomach tightens. I swallow back a wave of nausea. "Yes. Mostly."

"Wren." Gabriel turns around, head tilted to one side. "Be honest."

"He *is*." I sit up, wrapping my arms around my knees again. "He's a little . . . different, but it's him. It is, Gabriel. *He* is."

It's nearly four thirty, and the light outside is already dying. Backlit by the windows, Gabriel's face is hard to read—I can't make out more than the angular line of his profile and the hard set of his jaw. When he suddenly moves across the room to turn on a lamp, I'm startled, and I flinch when he drops down next to me on the sofa.

"Just tell me."

I take a deep breath. He's so close, there's only an afterthought of space between his thigh and my hip. The lamplight is a dirty gold puddle across the room, and in it the apartment looks even more like Early Fallout Shelter crossed with Garage Sale Reject.

I focus on a torn cardboard box spilling T-shirts and towels onto the faded floorboards. "I had to wait for a full moon. So I figured out when the next one would be and got everything I needed while I waited."

"What spell did you use?"

I flick my gaze sideways. "I wrote it myself."

His eyes widen. "Seriously?"

I shrug. "Seriously. I mean, I got my ideas from a few different books, but yeah."

His mouth is still hanging open a little when he makes a "go on" motion with one hand.

"I needed some things I couldn't find around here," I continue, staring at the toe of my boot over my knee. "Mandrake root. A ritual, um, blade. They call them—"

"Athames, I know. My grandmother had one she gave my mom when she died."

I swallow again. I wasn't expecting that. "I wrote it all out, and collected the other things I needed—saffron, poppy, hemlock. I sort of scoped out the cemetery a few nights before the full moon, to make sure no one would be around. And to, well, get used to it, you know?"

I shivered as I remembered those nights before the moon was due to rise full, and I sat near Danny's grave, sometimes resting my cheek on the simple stone, tracing the letters of his name, engraved in the marble. DANIEL FRANCIS GREER. I had never known his middle name was Francis.

"And on that night?" Gabriel sounds almost angry now.

"I was there at eleven, waiting for midnight. I had a picture of him, and a T-shirt of his, and all the other things. I had already blessed the athame, too."

I can feel the slight motion as he nods. "Then?"

I close my eyes to picture it. I don't think about it much anymore—it was hyper real at the time, too many sensations, the chill of the earth even in late July, the damp kiss of the grass on my knees, the flat, chalky smell of the stone, the dark blanket of sky overhead.

I had everything ready—a candle, a bowl and a small container of milk, the herbs, and the blade. I laid it all out, trying to ignore the way my hands shook, the faint crackling of squirrels in the trees, the grasshoppers' steady hum.

"At about five minutes to midnight, I poured the milk in the bowl and wrapped the mandrake root in Danny's shirt. I put that in the bowl, submerging it, and then added the saffron and the poppy and the hemlock." I glance at Gabriel, and his brow is twisted into a crooked, unhappy line.

"I laid the picture of him on the grave," I say, and my voice trembles a little then. It was a picture I loved—everything in it was perfectly Danny, from his Stooges T-shirt to the sun in his hair to the sleepy, soft smile on his face. "And I got out the knife."

"Shit, Wren."

I ignore him, plowing ahead, determined to get the rest of it out now. "I pricked my finger and smeared the blood on the picture. Then I cut my hand, here"—I hold out my right hand and show him the scar in the center of my palm—"and waited. As soon as it was midnight, I started the spell and squeezed my hand over the bowl."

I can remember the words even now, the smooth weight of them on my tongue, the sound of my voice in the silence. It had taken me almost a week to get it right, or as close to right as I thought it could be.

This night I seek to rekindle Life's bright fire
Fire stolen too soon by the cold grasp of Death
Untimely Death.

Spirits bright
Spirits dark
Spirits undecided and in between
Witness my invocation.

Life taken from you, Danny, return!
Love awaits you.
Death has no hold on you.

By candlelight
By starlight
By moonlight growing stronger
I command this to be.

With this symbol of Danny
With my blood
I command this to be.

Return to life
Return to me
Return to life
Return to me
Return to life
Return to me.

Gabriel closes his eyes and scrubs a hand over his face when I repeat the spell to him, and I bite my lip. It sounds wrong here in this shabby room, on the sofa that smells like ancient must and smoke. It sounds crazy, wrong and *crazy*, but I have to tell him the rest.

"I took the blade and drove it through his picture and into the ground, into the dirt." My heart is pounding now, remembering the racing thrill in my veins as I waited, the air in the graveyard swelling, pushing out, and the cool breeze that licked at the candle until it guttered and went out.

"And?" Gabriel says. He leans closer, folds his hand around my ankle again.

My voice is nothing more than a whisper. "I opened my eyes and Danny was there."

CHAPTER ELEVEN

IT'S NO PLACE TO STOP, BUT AS GABRIEL RAKES a hand through his hair again, my phone rings. It's Robin, so I can't ignore it.

"What?" I sound wrecked, even to my own ears.

"I can't find him and I looked everywhere! Are you coming home now? Wren?"

I can't make any sense of it, but then I picture Danny's face and my heart drops into my stomach without warning, a sickening *whoosh*. "Find who, Robin?"

"Mr. Purrfect! He's not anywhere in the house, and he won't come when I call, and you know he—"

"Robin." I sit back as my heart starts to beat again.

Of course she doesn't mean Danny. She doesn't even know about Danny; she wouldn't be looking for him. I'm totally losing it. "Calm down."

"Wren, he's *old*." She's panicking, which she almost never does, and she sounds about five years younger, the little Robin I remember, terrified in the middle of the night after a bad dream. "And he gets confused lately, and what if he's stuck somewhere or—"

"Hey, seriously, calm down. I'm coming home right now, okay? I'll be right there."

Gabriel is glaring at me when I flip the phone closed, and I shrug. "I have to go, it's my sister."

"We have to talk about this," he says, and folds his arms over his chest.

"Not right now we don't." I stand up and grab my backpack, hefting it over my shoulder.

I know I'm taking the easy way out, the perfect excuse to run away from the expression on Gabriel's face and the judgment in his eyes, but I don't care. It may be a relief not to have to lie about what I can do, what I have done, but I hadn't thought about how much disapproval would hurt. "Look, I get that you're worried or whatever—"

"Worried?" His laugh is a bark, short and sharp. "Are you kidding? You have your dead boyfriend living in your neighbor's garage!"

Power floods through me in a hot, aching rush, and across the room the lightbulb explodes beneath the lamp shade. "Back. Off."

I have to give him credit—he doesn't even flinch. But when he opens his mouth, I cut him off.

"I get it, okay? I really, really get it, believe me, and I've been living with this since July, instead of the last half hour. So just . . . back off already. I'm a big girl and I *will* deal with this. But first I have to find my sister's senile cat."

It's such a ridiculous thing to say, Gabriel snorts a laugh, and I can't help smiling. It breaks the tension in the room, soothes the angry hum of electricity in my blood.

When I head for the door, though, Gabriel grabs my hand. He turns it palm up and scrawls his phone number there with a blue ballpoint.

"Whenever you want," he says, and steps back.

And despite my big words, it's a relief to know he cares that much. But I'm pretty sure calling him might be a matter of need.

I drop my backpack by the front door and shrug off my jacket when I get home. "Robin?"

"In here." She appears in the door to the kitchen,

tears dried in silver tracks on her cheeks. Mr. Purrfect's favorite catnip mouse is clutched in one hand. She looks, well, like her beloved cat is missing, and my heart squeezes in sympathy even if I wish Mom hadn't let her give the beast such a completely lame name.

"Hey, come here." I open my arms and she walks straight into them, laying her head on my shoulder. The wet warmth of tears and snot is a little gross, but I stroke her hair anyway. "We'll find him, Binny. I promise."

I haven't called her that in years, and it makes her sniffle and heave a big, shuddering breath. "I know it's stupid. I know it. But he's getting old, Wren, and the Tates have that big, nasty dog—"

"Shhhh." I hold her closer and swallow a sigh. It's been a long time since the biggest crisis in my life was as simple as a cat who went out for an unsupervised walk, and I'm exhausted after Gabriel's interrogation. But Mom's at work, which leaves me to handle Robin, and the damn cat. Who hates me, not that that should matter.

I really hope it also doesn't matter that he followed me outside last night, since I can't remember seeing him again after that.

I let go of her when she seems a little calmer, and glance into the kitchen. Mr. Purrfect's bag of kibble looks like it exploded, clown-car-style—mounds of tiny fish-shaped pellets have spilled out of a bag half its size.

Robin winces when I look back at her. "I was shaking it, you know? To get him to come? And I was calling him and shaking it, and calling him, and . . . suddenly all this food started pouring out of it."

It's really coming, then, the moment when Robin can do the things I can do, and Mom can do, and for a second jealousy stabs at me. At least she has an idea it will happen to her, unlike me.

But that's something to deal with later. For now, we have to find the dumb cat.

"You checked the whole house?" I ask her, going back into the front hall to grab my jacket. "Closets, drawers, basement, everywhere?"

"Everywhere." She's practically vibrating with panic, and I don't blame her. The number of places a twelve-pound cat can hide is huge.

"He has to be outside, then. Come on."

She grabs a sweatshirt and follows me through the back door, already calling for him as she yanks it over her head. It's nearly dusk, the backyard crouching in the shadow of the scarred elm tree beside the garage.

"You check in there," I tell her, and squint into the gathering dark of the lawn, the space under the back steps, the scraggly bushes along the wall.

Robin knocks something over in the garage, and she comes out muttering and brushing off her sleeves. "If he's in there, he's somewhere I can't see. We need *light*."

The word is barely out of her mouth when a buttery glow follows the path of her outstretched hand. Her eyes widen, and I stumble backward a foot, but there's no time to comment on it because the light has fallen on a trampled path pressed into the dying grass.

Heading straight toward the corner of the yard, and Mrs. Petrelli's garage.

Robin's on her way before I can say anything, the yellow light wobbling in front of her. It's pretty clear that the path is too wide for a cat to have made, but she doesn't see that in her panic.

"Robin, slow down." I jog after her. "You might, um, scare him if he's back here."

"Mr. Purrfect," she calls, ignoring me. "C'mere, boy. Come on now, I've got dinner for you, boy." She's already at the break in the hedge, waving her hand to cast the light through the scraggly leaves.

And there, just on the other side of the hedge, is the cat, six feet from Mrs. Petrelli's garage, with a crumpled piece of paper in his mouth. His yellow eyes gleam hot when Robin's light bounces over his face.

"There you are!" The light disappears as she rushes

toward him, pushing through the leaves and dropping onto the grass with her hands outstretched. "Come here, boy."

I know it's not possible—if my heart really stopped, I would pass out, keel over, lose consciousness. But it feels that way as the stupid animal opens its mouth to mewl at her, dropping the paper on the ground at her knees.

All I can think is *wind*, but it's too late. Before the stiff breeze slaps at us, she picks up the paper and spreads it open. "What's this?" she says, petting the cat as he rubs against her thigh. His fur is standing partly on end, and I don't know if he's freaked out because of the wind or something else.

Like my dead boyfriend.

"Wren," Robin says as I stand there with my mouth open like an idiot. "It looks like one of Danny's."

The wrinkled page on her knees bears a cartoon sketch of a girl who looks just like me, in skinny black jeans and Docs, dark hair sticking out every which way, only half caught up in barrettes, and a bright red slash creating a smirk.

It is me, of course. And Robin would know—her favorite game was to get Danny to draw funny pictures for her, of me, of the cat, of himself, even of her. She still has a couple of them pinned to the wall over her desk, all signed with Danny's scribbled initials.

She loved him, too, and he treated her better than most boyfriends would treat someone's annoying little sister, because Danny was always willing to make someone smile.

None of that matters right now, though. I lean forward and snatch the paper off her lap. "Get the cat, come on. It's freezing."

"Where do you think he got that?" She stands up, Mr. Purrfect cradled in her arms and her voice muffled since she's speaking into his fur.

"I threw some stuff out the other day," I tell her, and glance back over my shoulder as we make our way across the yard. "It must have blown out of the trash."

She blinks, and even in the semidarkness I can read the betrayal on her face. "Oh."

It hurts to let the lie hang there, but there's nothing else I can do. Except glare at the cat, who hisses at me as Robin walks past on her way up the back steps.

"Turn it off," Danny says, frowning, when my phone buzzes for the fourth time.

It's Mom's late night at the salon—on Mondays she does bills and general cleanup after closing, so Robin and

I are on our own for dinner and homework. And since Robin locked herself in her room for some disgusting lovefest with the stupid cat after I made frozen pizza, I snuck out to the loft.

Darcia keeps texting me, though, little blips of happiness about Friday, and dumb stuff about school or home, just the way she used to. It's nice, except for how Danny—this Danny anyway—isn't used to sharing me.

"I can't." I stroke his back gently. He's sitting up, drawing something in the last of the big sketch pads I got him. "I told Robin I was going to the library, and Mom's not home, so I need to answer if she calls."

Now I'm lying to Danny, too. Not that I haven't been all this time, of course, but it feels different to lie to him about everyday things. I close my eyes for a second, swallowing back the instinct to start screaming and never stop.

He glances over his shoulder at me again, brow still creased. Three fat candles burn in the corner of the room on the floor, the flames casting dancing shadows over his face. For a moment, I'm sure I can see the blunt outline of his skull beneath his skin, the indentations of his eye sockets, and I shudder.

"Are you cold?" Just like that, his unhappiness is forgotten. He grabs the ratty quilt from the end of the mattress to tuck it around my legs, and his drawing falls to the floor.

It's nothing like his usual comic panels or figures. Instead, a huge, gnarled tree seems to grow out of the center of the page. The branches are bony, long arms that stretch into skeletal fingers, dozens of them reaching toward me as I stare at it, a twisted, funhouse tree.

I shudder again, and Danny moves closer, winding his arm around my waist. It doesn't help—he's like marble, cold and unforgiving, his ribs like a cage.

"What's that?" I ask him, pointing at the drawing while I try not to shiver.

He shrugs. "A tree. Can't you tell?"

"Well, yeah, but . . . you don't usually draw things like that." I reach into my pocket and pull out the folded sheet of paper, smoothing it open. "You usually draw stuff like this."

His sudden smile is startling, the Danny I love surfacing from under a shroud. "That's you. Yeah." Just as suddenly, he scowls. "I had to throw it at the cat."

I actually gulp, shaking now. "The cat?"

"Robin's cat." He moves away, body tight with tension again, the line of his back a blunt backslash in the candlelight. "Stupid thing hates me now. It used to like me."

I nearly tear the paper as I sit up straight, pushing the blanket away and touching his arm. "When was the cat up here, Danny?"

The noise he makes is dismissive, like it's no big deal. "Before. Hissed and showed his claws. I used to give him tuna, man. It's not right."

Oh God. Oh God, oh God, oh *God*. "Danny, did you leave the stairs down?"

"I can hear you coming better when I do," he says, and gives me the sweetest smile. Wide, bright, completely honest—I saw that smile so often, when we met in the parking lot after school, or when he would look up from drawing as I studied on the sofa, or when he lifted his head from the pillows on his bed, flushed and already sleepy.

For a moment, I want to reach out and trace his lips with my fingers, relearn the generous curve of his mouth, but I know if I do the moment will be ruined. Danny's mouth is too cool now, lips not as soft as they used to be, and it's always a reminder. Danny—my Danny—is gone. What I brought back is just an imitation.

Instead I close my fingers gently around his wrist, my thumb stroking the place where his pulse used to be. "You can't do that, Danny. Remember? We talked about that. It's not safe."

His smile disappears as quickly as it broke open, and when he leans closer, I realize I'm stiff with fear.

"But you're not here," he says, a low whisper. "You're not here so much, Wren. I need you here, I keep telling you, when you're not here I can't *think*, Wren, I can't, it's all cloudy, and I see the tree, and I smell the smoke, and I can't *think*—"

My hand is shaking when I reach up to touch his mouth, stopping the furious flow of words. He's trembling, too, something fierce and frantic coursing through him, and I have to stop this, I have to do something.

For now, all I can do is stroke his cheek and murmur, "Sleep now, Danny, sleep. I'm right here, sleep, sleep . . ."

It takes a few minutes for it to work tonight, and he clings to my free hand the whole time, icy fingers gripping tight. When he finally lies down, I pet his hair for a few minutes before slipping free.

At the bottom of the stairs, I use the broomstick to push them up into place, listening for the heavy *snick* that means they're shut tight. And all the way across the dark lawn, my heart thumps wildly as I remember what he said about the tree and the smoke.

He's talking about the tree in his drawing. It's the tree that was torn open in the car crash. The tree that killed him.

CHAPTER TWELVE

ANOTHER LONG NIGHT OF BAD DREAMS MUST
show on my face, because the next morning Mom hovers.
Standing too close, squinting at me over her coffee—
considering, wondering, suspecting.

I try to keep my head down as I gulp my own coffee.
I haven't given Mom any of my laundry in days, and I'm
wearing my least favorite sweater and a denim miniskirt
I hate. Mom knows it, too, because she lifted an eyebrow
when I walked into the kitchen, my hair still wet and
sticking up in a dozen directions.

She doesn't even make a pointed comment about
keeping up with the wash, though, which is so unlike

her, *I'm* suspicious.

Robin's chattering enough for everyone, as usual, splashing milk over her cereal and, I realize halfway into my caffeine, telling Mom all about Mr. Purrfect's big adventure. I nearly spit out my coffee when she says, "And then we found him way out back, like he'd been in Mrs. Petrelli's yard."

It doesn't really mean anything—he's a cat, he can and will wander anywhere—but anything that draws attention to the garage is a bad thing. And I'm only making it worse, since Mom is frowning at me like I've grown a second head.

"Wren?"

"Coffee went down the wrong way," I say, and give her a weak smile before I grab my backpack. "I'm working tonight, so I won't be home till late."

I'm out the front door before she can answer, but as I walk to school I can picture the look on her face, curious instead of worried, at least for now.

I just hope I can keep it that way.

School is torture. Gabriel is waiting in homeroom, gray eyes trained on me the minute I walk in, and I mouth, *Later,* as I glare at him. I can't talk about Danny now, and definitely not here. Gabriel's frustration is almost tangible, crowding hot against me.

I see Ryan in the hall outside my chemistry room, which is always awkward, and by the time I get to lunch, where Jess is waiting, I've never been more tempted to run away. Or simply curl up in a ball and howl, right there on the grimy floor. Jess is bubbly with gossip and plans for Friday night—something about renting some new vampire flick—and I can hardly do more than nod and try to smile.

The thought of Danny is like a sore tooth all day, wondering if he's safely in the loft the way he's supposed to be, dreading how much of the accident he's beginning to remember. Every lie and half-truth seems to burn just under my skin, and when I walk into Bliss after school, Trevor takes one look at me and barks, "What the hell is wrong with you?"

It takes every ounce of willpower I have not to blast him off his stool with the simple force of my fury. I stalk into the kitchen and throw my backpack on the floor in the corner instead. "Your boyfriend is a real humanitarian, you know that?"

Geoff sighs and looks up from the sandwiches left over from lunch, which he's boxing up for the shelter in Plainfield. "I'll send him out with these, huh? He's in a mood today."

Geoff leaves me alone once Trevor is gone, but he puts in one of my favorite CDs as I wipe down tables and organize the mess that Trevor always leaves behind the counter. After a few minutes, I relax into the mindlessness of the work, making lattes and espresso, serving Geoff's awesome carrot cake, and calling back to him for one of the salads he makes to order. It's not incredibly busy, but there are enough customers to keep me occupied and moving, which is perfect.

Bliss has always been a sort of haven for me, even before I got the job. It still sports the building's original tin ceiling, painted silver now, and the exposed brick wall along the east side of the room is a faded red, worn with time and touch. None of the tables and chairs match, but Geoff painted them all the same chocolate brown and trimmed them with either bright green or purple. Framed art for sale hangs everywhere, and there's a stand with indie CDs and local authors' books. Everything Trevor lacks when it comes to dealing with actual human beings apparently went into a green thumb, so he keeps spider plants and ferns all over, and the café always feels comfortable, warm, alive.

I'm enjoying the calm when the bell over the door jingles and Gabriel walks in.

I manage to trip over my boot and drop my squirt

bottle of window cleaner at the same time in my surprise. Geoff's putting a fresh tray of cookies in the bakery case and raises an eyebrow when Gabriel bends down to pick up the bottle for me. Great. Like I need another member of the judging panel.

Geoff loved Danny. Everyone loved Danny, really, but Geoff was always happy when Danny came in, and sometimes let him hang around in the back and sketch while he was baking if my shift wasn't over. He and Trevor actually came to the funeral, closed the café and everything, and Geoff hung a couple of Danny's drawings behind the counter where everyone who's getting coffee can see them.

"I can't talk now, either," I hiss at Gabriel, and grab the bottle away from him.

"Can't I get a coffee? Jeez." Gabriel ambles over to the counter, and I sigh as I follow him.

"You didn't come here just for coffee," I say as soon as Geoff disappears into the kitchen again.

"No, but I still want some." He shrugs, his shoulders all angles in his faded blue button-down and green hoodie, a pale sheaf of his hair falling across his forehead. I don't know why I keep noticing things like that, because they don't matter. Not to me. They *don't*.

"Fine. What can I get you?"

"Regular, two sugars," he says after scanning the

menu on the chalkboard for way too long.

I soften a little at that. It's the cheapest coffee we offer, and after yesterday I know he probably doesn't have a lot of extra money for lattes or anything else. I slap a black-and-white cookie on a plate and don't charge him for it, because I know Geoff won't care.

Anyway, I owe Gabriel. It's a relief not to have to lie to him, at least, even if I'm pretty sure what he wants to talk about isn't something I'm going to want to hear.

"I just want to help," he says softly as he takes the mug and the plate, and I look up to find those strange gray eyes trained on me again.

"I know." I swipe at the counter with my rag absently. "I'm sorry."

"What time do you get off?"

"Not till nine. Sometimes a little earlier if it's slow." I wave a hand at Rich from the movie theater when he walks in, and Gabriel takes a step backward.

"I'll come back around eight then, okay? Maybe walk you home?"

It's the only way we can talk, since I'm not about to invite him over, and there are too many curious eyes on us at school.

I just won't think about the fact that it might be kind of nice, too.

★ ★ ★

"Got a date, huh?" Trevor says at eight, when Gabriel has passed by the front window for the fifth time. He's hunched into a warmer jacket, and he's got even cheaper coffee from the diner over on North in one hand.

"Hardly," I snap, and push chairs into place with an angry screech on the bare wood floor. The café is already empty, and Geoff always leaves at dinnertime.

"Hey, I'm not judging."

My head snaps up at that, and I find him slouched against the bakery case, his face as thoughtful as it ever gets. I open my mouth to answer him, but I can't think of anything to say. Of all the people I thought might be cool about me possibly talking to another boy, Trevor was last on my list.

"Look, you had it rough," Trevor says, and his voice is softer than I've ever heard it. "It's hard when somebody you love dies. I know, believe me. But life goes on. I mean, that's what they say, right? And it's true."

I'm so stunned, my mouth is hanging open. Trevor's not even looking at me anymore, sifting through the receipts behind the counter instead, and after a minute, he keeps talking.

"When you love someone, the last thing you want is for them to be unhappy. And I think that's true even when you die. I mean, if I died, I wouldn't want Geoff to pine forever. A few months, sure, I mean, I'm worth that at least, but I'd hate the idea of him moping around forever, staring at my pictures and baking himself into oblivion."

Is that what he thinks I'm doing? Is that what everyone else really expects? Me, a teenage widow, in love with Danny, dead Danny, forever and ever, end of story? God, if any of them knew what I'd done instead . . .

I'm still gaping when Trevor looks up, his gaze sharp and far more knowing than I ever imagined. Maybe someone he loved died a long time ago. Maybe other people have actually gone through this without going insane and casting dark spells at midnight.

"I think we're done, Wren. If anyone else comes in, I can handle it. Go on home. And take a fresh coffee to your friend out there when you go."

I'm not about to argue. I'm still too shocked to form words anyway, and when I tap Gabriel on the shoulder outside ten minutes later, he's just as surprised to see me there.

"You could have come in, you know," I say, and wrap my scarf around my neck. The wind is biting, and there's no moon, just a faint dusting of stars.

"I didn't want to get you in trouble."

I try to ignore the blush creeping up the back of my

neck, even in the cold. He's flirting; there's no way to deny it.

And it feels good. There's no denying that, either.

We drink our coffee in silence for a few minutes as we walk past the bookstore and the dry cleaner's and the drugstore. The movie theater on the corner is all lit up, and I wave at Nan Bernstein, who's leaning on the counter of the ticket booth, beyond bored.

"Friend?" Gabriel asks as we cross the street.

I shrug. "I've known her since kindergarten. It's a pretty small town in some ways."

"I noticed." His tone is dry. "I got a lot of 'back off' vibes when I was asking about you yesterday."

That's surprising. I've lived here all my life, but I don't have many friends, not close ones anyway. Danny did, though, and they were all pretty loyal.

I swallow the last of my coffee and toss the cup in a trash can outside the video store. "What about you? What about where you were from, before?"

Even in the dark I can see his jaw tighten, the hard line of it nearly forming a right angle. "We've lived a lot of places," he says finally. "None of them for too long."

It's not fair that he can see into me so easily, when reading him seems to require a whole new language. I may not love my hometown, but it's what I know, and even if I don't intend to stick around here forever, it's comfortable, even comforting in its own way. I didn't meet Danny till high school, but we still shared the same memories of ice cream at Hill's in the summer, sledding in the park, the Memorial Day parade with the fire trucks all shined up.

I can't imagine a series of houses, and especially not grungy little apartments like the one Gabriel's sharing with his sister now. When everything else is exploding, I know I can go *home*, to a place as familiar to me as my own face, where the Christmas tree will stand lopsided in the same corner every year and the bathroom faucet will always drip and the attic will always smell faintly of lavender and ancient pipe tobacco.

"Is here better?" I ask without thinking, and he turns to me with a sudden smile.

"It is now."

CHAPTER THIRTEEN

IT'S TOO COLD TO SIT OUTSIDE. AT LEAST THAT'S what I tell myself as Gabriel leads me up to his apartment again. Olivia's at work, he says, and she wouldn't mind anyway, and I tell myself that we're only going to talk, that being alone together like this doesn't mean anything.

It still feels wrong, though, when Gabriel unlocks the door, and I bump into his back as he searches for the light switch. His clothes are cold, but I can feel the warmth underneath them, the faint thump of his heart, and for a minute I'm tempted to hang on, to bury my face between his shoulder blades and just cry, and that's so wrong.

Instead, I stumble away from him and cling to my

backpack like it's going to save me from doing something crazy. "I can't stay too long. I have homework and stuff, and my mom knows when I get off."

I don't say that I'm worried about Danny, alone since last night, maybe just as restless as he was then, maybe more. I also don't say that I've already rationalized that if Trevor hadn't let me go early, I wouldn't have been able to get to the loft now anyway.

You could have gone straight there, the nasty voice that I've come to hate whispers in my head. *Mom won't expect you for almost an hour. You could be with him right now.*

I squeeze my eyes shut, ignoring it, trying to get myself together as Gabriel turns on another lamp and strips off his jacket. When I hear the heavy canvas hit the floor, I breathe out. I'm being stupid. I hate being stupid. We're only going to talk, and if I'm lucky, Gabriel will know things that can help me.

I don't want to think about what he might be able to help me do, though, not yet. One thing at a time.

"You want something to drink?" he says, and I start at the sound of his voice, suddenly a lot nearer than I imagined.

I turn around and he's right there, head cocked to one side. "I'm good, thanks." My voice trembles a little, and it makes me furious.

But I'm not nervous because of Gabriel. I'm not scared of him. I'm scared of myself, and the fact that I like being close to him as much as I do. If I closed my eyes again right now, I know I could feel the Gabriel from my dream, the heat of his chest under my cheek, the weight of his hand on my back.

I take a step backward, and the back of my calf smacks the coffee table so hard it wobbles. Gabriel's nice enough to pretend not to notice, though, and instead gently disentangles my backpack from my hands.

"Take your coat off and sit down?"

I nod, hoping I can manage that without looking like a complete moron. He slouches next to me, and for a minute we're silent.

"So," he finally says, and takes a deep breath. "You raised your boyfriend from the dead."

I wince. "I had nothing to do that night?"

"Wren, it's not funny."

I groan and sink into the sofa, tilting my head back to stare at the ceiling. There's a stain on the plaster in the shape of a rabbit's foot. Does that mean Gabriel is going to bring me good luck? I doubt it.

"I know it's not funny, okay? I know exactly how funny it isn't, and I've known since that night. It just hurt so much, Gabriel, you don't even know. And I . . ." I stop and twist my head to look him in the eye. "I'm not sure I really expected it to work, you know? I mean, I did, but I didn't. And I definitely didn't think about what would happen afterward. All I wanted was to see him again, touch him again. When he appeared in the graveyard, I thought my heart would stop. I hadn't even thought about what would happen next, you know? And now . . ." My voice trails off in the silence, a little wisp of sound that shames me.

"Now you have your dead boyfriend living in your neighbor's garage."

"God, stop it!" I sit up, knocking into him with my elbow. "I told you, I get it. And if all you're going to do is sit there all Judgey McJudgerson and tell me things I already know, then fuck you."

He grabs my arm before I can get up, pulling me back down onto the sofa and holding my hand tight. "Stop. I'm sorry. It's just a lot to wrap your head around, you know? For anybody who's not you, it takes a little repeating just to believe it."

"But you saw," I whisper, and swallow hard as I look at him.

He nods, and the motion is weighted with sadness. "I saw. Wren, magic like that is serious stuff. It's dark arts all the way. It means . . ." It's his turn to leave the sentence unfinished, and he stares at our tangled hands while he thinks.

"What?" I say when he's silent too long. "What does it mean?"

"You're powerful." His eyes are slate now, darker than I've ever seen them. "I can feel it inside you, and it's big. Really big, and that's a little scary. My grandmother died a long time ago, but my mom told me some stories about her, and I don't think she could have done what you did, you know?"

The *not that she would have tried* goes unspoken.

I wrench my hand out of his and stand up, and even though my legs are suddenly a little shaky, I pace back and forth. "It's not something I asked for, Gabriel. We . . ." It's another secret, maybe a bigger one, but he has to know, even if telling it feels like the worst kind of betrayal. "The women in my family can all do this. Magic, the craft, whatever you want to call it. All of them. Robin's almost there right now. And my mother . . ."

I can't say any more, not yet. Even the little I've admitted has left a bitter taste in my mouth. I've never said any of this aloud, to anyone, and now Gabriel knows it all, this boy I met a week ago.

This boy who's looking at me like a puzzle he wants

to solve, but one he'll enjoy working on for as long as it takes.

I can't decide if that's good or bad, but at the moment it doesn't really matter.

"What about your mother?" he asks, leaning forward, his elbows on his knees. His hands are clasped together loosely, his long, tapered fingers more elegant than Danny's.

Stop it. God, like that matters.

"She's never talked to me about it." I stop pacing and stand still, letting my head fall forward. I'm so tired. It probably sounds like everything is simply spilling out of me, but it feels like I'm dragging it out bit by bit, all of it heavy and awkward, bumping and scraping against my heart as I release it. "She's got just as much power as I do, but she refuses to use it most of the time. And she doesn't talk to my aunt anymore, I think because of it."

"So what happened when you first started feeling the power?" Gabriel is frowning, fierce. I take a step backward instinctively.

"She just sort of brushed it under the rug, so to speak. Robin and I have both seen her do things all our lives, but mostly the results of it, you know?" I rub my temples, trying to think of how to explain it. "She doesn't actually *do* it in front of us really, or not often, but if something's broken it will suddenly be fixed, or the fire will keep burning all afternoon. Stuff like that."

"So you never knew what it meant, or how to do anything, you just figured it out on your own?" He's on his feet now, striding past me, and for a minute I'm sure he's going to storm out the door to confront my mother.

But he's only pacing, too, even if his hands are balled into fists.

"It sounds bad, I know," I begin, and he rolls his eyes.

"Bad? It sounds pretty frigging cruel, if you ask me."

Out of nowhere, an urge to protect Mom unfurls in a wash of electricity that blues the light in the room. Gabriel shuts his mouth, but I can tell he's not really sorry.

"You don't know her." My voice is carefully controlled now, even though it crackles with a leftover spark of power. "You don't know us. And this isn't about what she did or didn't teach me. It was no one's idea but mine to bring Danny back, and it's no one's job but mine to take care of it."

It hurts to say that, like Danny is a bag of trash that needs to be put out on the curb. It's still true, though.

"I'm sorry, okay?" He comes closer, slowly, and I take a deep breath, tamping down the last vibrating hum of energy inside. And when he takes my hands in his, my first instinct isn't to run, or to lash out, it's to hold tight.

He waits for a minute, his eyes searching my face, before he speaks again. "I just want to help, Wren. You have to know this isn't going to have a happy ending. I mean, doesn't he ask about his family? About his friends?"

"He didn't at first." My voice is so small, even I can barely hear it. "At first, he was happy just to be with me. But then he started to remember things. To want things, other things." I turn my face up to him, and I can't hide the tears burning in my eyes. "I didn't think about this part. I just wanted him *back*."

"I know." He's so close, I can smell the night air clinging to his clothes and his hair. "I'm just afraid of what might happen now."

"He would never hurt me." I'm too quick to say it, and I wonder if Gabriel can tell that I don't completely believe it anymore.

"But he can't live up in that garage forever, Wren. You know that, right?"

"Of course I know it!" I wrestle my hand free and step back, wiping an escaped tear from one cheek with the back of my hand. "That was a last-minute thing. And I told you, I'm going to figure this out. Just . . . not tonight."

"You can't put it off, Wren." He steps closer again, and I back up. I can't think when he's so near, so warm.

"Well, first I have to pass my chemistry test and get through Friday night," I mutter.

"What's Friday night?"

I huff out a laugh that's mostly a sigh, and shake my head. "A sleepover. A stupid girly sleepover at my house, because my friends are ready to walk out of my life forever, and I can't bear it if that happens, so I have to sit through some horror movie and eat popcorn and watch Jess paint her nails, okay?"

He doesn't look convinced, but I'm not interested in making him understand. Not right now.

"Wren, let me help, okay? I could do some research. I don't want you to go through this alone. And I really don't want you to get hurt."

He's serious, and everything about the defined angles of his body is softer now. But I can't help blurting out, "God, why do you care?"

He flinches as if I slapped him. "Isn't it obvious? I noticed *you* before I picked up on your power, Wren."

That shouldn't feel as good as it does, a bright hot pulse in my chest. It doesn't matter if Gabriel likes me, and it really doesn't matter if I like Gabriel. There's Danny to think about. Always Danny.

I don't know what to say, so I stand there blinking instead, and finally Gabriel gives up and takes a step toward me again. I don't back up this time, even though I do have to tilt my head to look him in the eye. Why are the only boys who like me always so tall?

"I saw *you*, Wren," Gabriel says, and his voice is so soft, a feather drifting on the air, that I close my eyes to listen. "I saw this girl with these dark eyes and this crazy hair and this *fuck you* look on her face, and I wanted to talk to you."

I laugh and open my eyes. "Wow. Smooth."

He smirks, his mouth twisting to one side, and shrugs a little. "It's true. You don't look like everybody else, and that's a good thing."

"At least the outside and the inside match," I say, and let myself move just a little closer. I can't help it—my life has become a series of balls I'm trying to keep in the air, and I can't hold on to any of them long enough.

I want to hold on to Gabriel.

My hands find his forearms, and I tangle my fingers in the worn cotton of his sleeves. Another kick of energy washes through me, warm and bright, and the air shimmers around us. I want so much, so much I can't have, so much I'm not supposed to even think about.

But I stretch up anyway, trembling, hearing the echo of Gabriel's voice: *I saw you. I saw you.*

I never thought I wanted to be seen like that, so

completely. I didn't think it was possible, after keeping so many secrets for so long. It's amazing how good it feels.

When I press my mouth to Gabriel's, I can feel the shimmer, taste it, sweet, mellow gold where our lips touch, a slow-blooming heat that twines around us like vines. And it's so bittersweet, so much like that long-ago first kiss with Danny, I break away with a jerk.

"I have to go," I manage to get out, and then I'm scrambling, pushing away from Gabriel's outstretched hands and the sound of his voice to grab my stuff and run.

CHAPTER FOURTEEN

DANNY WAS A SECRET FOR A LITTLE WHILE.
Before he died, I mean. He didn't have to be—it's not
like my mom was opposed to me having a boyfriend,
even though I had to sit through the big sex talk after we
got serious, which was epically awkward. I never thought
I would hear my mom say "condom" so many times,
although watching her unwrap one did make us both
giggle, since she'd somehow managed to buy fluorescent
ones.

I stopped her before she made me put it on a banana,
though.

I wasn't really worried about Jess and Darcia, either.

We'd talked about boys since sixth grade, after all, starting with Bailey Sutter, who got tall before any of the other boys, and used to bump into Jess at every opportunity, which was as close to a declaration of love as you got at twelve.

Danny wasn't the first boy I'd crushed on, but he was the first boy I couldn't stop thinking about, the first one who made me itchy and nervous waiting for the phone to ring, the first one I wanted to climb all over, climb *inside*, take apart so I could see and touch every part of him.

I didn't want to share him. It was a little bit like drawing a picture—I didn't want anyone to see it until I was finally happy with it. And being with him those first few weeks was just as magical as learning what I could do had been, touching a flower and watching the color deepen, swooping the music on my iPod higher with a gesture. I was giddy with the way I could look at him across the cafeteria, find him smiling at me, and know that he was mine, that this huge thing that had happened to me was still *just* mine. No one could question it or taint it or ruin it—I could hold it, perfect and whole, as long as I wanted.

It didn't last, of course. After a while, it got too hard not to let him take my hand in the hallway, or snug up behind me at my locker, his chin balanced on the top of my head as his hands snaked around my waist. After a while I wanted to share it, to show it off, to let the world see why I was smiling like a complete idiot half the time.

It's not like that with Gabriel.

My phone buzzes that night, after I've run the last few windy blocks home, the taste of him still on my lips and my cheeks hot with shame and guilt. I know I should probably ignore it, but I don't. I curl up under the covers instead, staring out the window as the bare branches of the tree outside scrape at the sky, and answer it.

It's another secret, another lie, and the worst part is that I'm lying to myself this time. Telling myself that I'm only talking to Gabriel because there's no one else, and because he might be able to help me figure out what to do about Danny. Ignoring the rushing shiver when I remember kissing him, pretending that I don't wish we were in the same room so I could do it again.

"I'm falling asleep," I whisper into the phone after an hour of talking about things that don't matter, music and pizza and Mr. Rokozny's horrible suits and the costumes we wore on Halloween as kids.

"And my phone is dying," he says. I can hear his smile.

"Okay. Well . . ." I don't know what to say then, and I don't really want to say good-bye. The sound of his voice is an anchor, bobbing sure and steady across the crackling connection, and I want to hold on to it for as long as I can.

"It's okay, Wren. I'll see you tomorrow." I can hear him breathing, the distant rustle of fabric that means he must be in bed, too. "It's really okay."

I want it to be. I want a lot of things that I'm not going to get, though, so I tell him, "It's really not," and click off the phone before I start to cry.

I'm pulled in every direction the next two days, stretched so tight I'm sure I'll snap and tear. On Wednesday Madame Hobart looks like someone just drowned every kitten in the world, and apparently decides torture by the past imperfect tense is the answer to her mood. We get hit with a compare-and-contrast essay on *The Stranger* in World Lit, and I fail the chem lab so spectacularly I'm amazed nothing gets blown up.

It doesn't help that Jess is there at lunch, tossing stray vegetables from her salad onto my tray and pulling nail polishes out of her bag to hold up for my inspection. Dar's got a playlist ready for Friday night and a plan to make double fudge brownies, and meanwhile Gabriel is watching me in the hall and in class, eyes shifting to his notebook whenever I catch him or when Jess and Dar are around.

Mom needs me at the salon after school on Wednesday, too, because two of the girls are out sick, and she steers me between the phones and the broom and the wet mess of used towels waiting for the washer. By the time we're in the car on the way home I have three texts from Dar, two from Jess, and six from Gabriel, and Mom raises an eyebrow as I thumb through them.

"Missing some big party this afternoon?" she says as she pulls into the driveway. The car's engine dies with a grunt and a wheeze, and she tilts her head to one side, waiting as I flip my phone shut.

"Oh yeah. Rock stars, limos, crazy drugs. The usual Wednesday afternoon scene." I'm aiming for sarcastic but I land on tired instead, and she reaches out to stroke my cheek.

"You okay, babe?"

I swallow as I look up at her. Her face is so familiar, the slender nose, the delicate mouth, all that thick hair the color of healthy bark, even the smell of her, clean cotton and magnolia over the faint tang of hair dye. For a second I want to admit that I'm not, that I need her to fix everything and let me sleep for about a month, and before I can stop it I'm seeing her through the sting of tears.

"Hey." She leans closer, runs her thumb over my

cheekbone and my jaw, a whispering touch. "What's going on?"

I shake my head and pull away. I can't give in. I don't want to know what would happen if she found out about Danny. It's too enormous to even imagine, like the whole earth going up in a ball of flame. "I'm just tired," I say, and stuff my phone in my bag as I reach for the door handle. "I didn't sleep well last night."

She doesn't believe me—I can see it in her eyes—but it's actually not far from the truth. I dreamed all night, of the tree where Becker's car crashed, wrapping its spindly limbs around me until I couldn't breathe, of Danny wandering into Bliss, his skin gray and torn, his eyes as dead as the stones that fell out of his pockets, and the whole café full, my mother and Jess and Gabriel and Trevor, all waiting for me to see him, turning me around to watch as he wept blood onto the counter.

My subconscious isn't very subtle, I guess.

Thursday's not a lot better, especially since I was up until two again, trying to convince Danny I had to go home. I'm so tired I feel brittle, and I snap at Alicia Ferris in the hall after history when she takes a picture of me picking up notebooks and my iPod and crushed packs of gum from my dropped backpack.

"Seriously?" I hiss, blinking away the flash and

feeling that dangerous knife edge of anger cutting through my control. I'm crouched awkwardly with a partially unwrapped tampon in one hand and a forgotten, desiccated apple in the other.

"It's for the yearbook," she says, smirking, and holds up the camera to take another.

That's it—I haven't even thought about what I'd like to do when the power rolls up out of me in a tingling wave, and the sprinkler above Alicia's head bursts to life. I scuttle backward, out of the line of fire, as she shrieks and drops the camera.

People up and down the hall are shouting and laughing, and within seconds Andy Petrov is in his socks, sliding along the wet floor, shaking his head like a puppy. Alicia is still stunned and soaked through, ignoring the smashed camera to peel her wet clothes away from her body. Mascara drips down her cheeks like black tears.

By the time Principal Gorder turns the corner, the sprinkler is spitting to a stop and I'm halfway down the hall to lunch. I'm not tired anymore, but I feel scooped out, empty, and beneath the satisfaction—I've hated Alicia since fourth grade, at least—the guilt is already rolling inside like a sour stomach.

Jess is waiting, as usual now, and I only manage a quick glance at Gabriel before I sit down at the table she's chosen. He gives me a small smile before holding up his phone, and the brief flare of relief in my chest somehow feels worse on top of the guilt. There will be a text from him, then, and I hate how much I want to see it, how much I want school to be over so I can talk to him, instead of plotting tomorrow night's fun with Jess.

By the time I meet Gabriel behind the public library a half hour after school is over, I'm back to exhausted. I can't even think about the essay I have to write, or the new trig problems, even though I know my grades are slipping. College seems like a distant impossibility today, and one that matters a lot less than the next twenty-four hours.

"Hey." Gabriel is slouched against the faded red brick, and he stands up when I round the corner of the building. I never got closer than five feet away from him yesterday, and I don't even bother to argue with myself as I walk straight into his arms. We connect with a vague *oomph*. I don't think he was expecting that, but I don't care.

Judging by the way his arms go around me, sliding under my backpack, he doesn't either.

"Bad day?" His words are muffled by my hair.

"Bad night," I tell him, and pull away far enough to look up at him.

His voice sharpens. "What happened?"

"Don't be a big damn hero, okay?" I poke his chest with one finger. "Just be my friend."

"You didn't answer the question."

I sigh. "I know."

I don't want to, which is the first problem. Not because I'm afraid Gabriel will go all tough guy, but because it hurts to admit that Danny is getting harder and harder for me to control.

Last night when I finally snuck out there, he was down in the garage, prowling around near the door to the yard. Thin and pale in the sliver of light through the window, he looked like something from another world when he turned around and saw me standing there, my mouth hanging open and my heart pumping pure terror.

He didn't even smile the way he used to. When I think about it, he hasn't in days. Instead, he focuses those flat dark eyes on me, as if now he can see into me, too, and he wants something there that he can grab onto and twist, viciously.

I wriggle out of Gabriel's hold and kick aside some damp leaves to sit down with my back to the cool brick. Gabriel joins me, his knee brushing mine.

"Do you want to talk about it?"

"Not really." I shrug, and he winds his arm around my shoulders. The weight of it is a comfort, and I let my head rest against it. "I had to make up a spell last night just so I could leave. It was terrifying—I was trying to remember what I'd read in some of the books and figure out what to say, and all I could think was that I didn't want to make things worse."

"What do you mean, so you could leave?"

I stare at my lap, where my battered backpack is covered with Danny's doodles, faded Sharpie initials and faces. "He doesn't like being alone anymore. So when I need to leave, he gets . . . upset."

It's an understatement for the stubborn way Danny held on to me last night, wrapped around me from behind, his chin digging into my shoulder, his voice low and cold in my ear.

"Wren." Gabriel stiffens beside me, and I reach up to grab his hand, twining my fingers with his.

"I'm going to figure it out, I promise. And he's not going to hurt me, Gabriel. He wouldn't."

I wish I was actually sure of that. I wish I had any idea what "figuring it out" meant. Just the thought of doing something to hurt him is enough to make me ill. I'm not strong enough to strangle him or smother him, and he isn't actually breathing anyway, so what good would that do?

The fact that I'm sitting here in the chilly leaves

imagining ways to get rid of the boy I loved so much I brought him back from the dead is so ridiculous, so horrifying, it's almost funny. In an unbelievable, black humor way that's not really funny at all.

"I wish I believed that," Gabriel says, and rests his head against mine, kissing my hair gently.

I can't tell him that Danny was down in the garage last night, way too close to venturing outside. I can't tell him that with Danny's arms around me last night, it had been hard to breathe, harder still to concentrate on winging a makeshift spell with my ribs crushed under Danny's forearms.

"I just have to get through tomorrow night," I say instead. "This weekend, I'm going to . . . well, I don't know what, but I'll figure something out. And then . . ."

I don't know where that sentence should end. Then what? We can stop hiding? We can date? I can pretend that I didn't make the most horrible mistake you can make in the name of love and get on with kissing the cute new guy?

I don't deserve a happy ending. I don't even deserve a semi-happy ending, because Danny isn't going to get one. He might have—he might have been in heaven, for all I know, lounging around in his favorite T-shirt with his guitar making the kind of noises he couldn't quite get it to make while he was alive and pinning his drawings to the clouds. I took that away from him. So I could have him back, so I wouldn't be alone.

And now, somehow, I'm going to be the one to end his life, again. Kiss of death, that's me.

"Hey," Gabriel says, and nuzzles the top of my head. "And then, okay? Just concentrate on there being a then."

"I know." I twist around so I can look up at him, the bricks scraping against my back, and find him right there, waiting. There aren't any more words, not right now, so I kiss him again.

He tastes sweet, and the soft give of his mouth feels like coming home. I lick the curve of his bottom lip before I pull away, and he shudders out a breath and tightens his arm around me before resting his forehead on mine.

Then feels impossibly far away.

CHAPTER FIFTEEN

"HEY, ARE YOU LISTENING?"

I drag my gaze away from the window in the butler's pantry, where I'm holed up with my phone. The yard is dark in the shadow of the trees, and I can barely make out the outline of Mrs. Petrelli's garage.

"I'm here, sorry. Just trying to figure out this last trig problem." It's a lie, of course, but Jess will buy it. I'm worse at trig than she is.

"Wren, it's almost midnight. Do it tomorrow. Or skip it and beg mercy from Ms. Nardini. She'll let you off if you just gush about her knockoff Louboutins."

"Oh yeah, because I really look like the type to be

craving Louboutins of my very own," I say, rolling my eyes. The windowsill is digging into my forearm as I press my nose to the glass and squint into the thick blackness outside. There's barely a moon tonight.

Mom didn't go up to bed until almost eleven, and I heard the low hum of her TV for a half hour after that. I had just crept down the stairs to the kitchen when Jess called. I'd forgotten my phone was in the pocket of my hoodie, and it sounded so shrill in the silence, I'd flipped it open without thinking.

And wound up here, huddled in the butler's pantry, which Mom uses as storage for pretty much anything she doesn't want to haul up from the basement or find cluttered in the hall—Christmas lights, Robin's sports stuff, the box from the new toaster, lightbulbs. At least there's a window.

"All I know is, no homework talk tomorrow night," Jess says sternly. "Even from Dar. I know she's freaking about her lit project, but I am not discussing dead nineteenth-century white men on a Friday night."

I just hope we're not discussing dead twenty-first-century ones instead.

"Speaking of Friday, it's after midnight now." I yawn, trying to make it sound natural. "I have to go to bed."

"Me too." Jess sighs. "Okay, see you tomorrow. And

if you think of anything you want me to bring tomorrow night, tell me at lunch, huh?"

"Gotcha," I say, and click the phone shut the moment we say good-bye.

It's cold tonight, colder than it's been for weeks, and I shiver in my hoodie as I run across the yard and slip through the hedge. My heart is already a loose fist, knocking clumsy and hard in my chest. I hate being nervous when I climb the stairs now, but Danny has changed so much since that first night, kneeling beside me in the cemetery, clinging and kissing and smiling the smile I loved so much.

A stray branch smacks my thigh as I wriggle through, and I stop in my tracks. The side door to the garage is wide open, and as I watch, it creaks wider in the wind. *No.*

"Danny," I whisper as I run inside. The stairs are pulled down; the broomstick I've used to push them up into place the last few days is snapped in half on the gritty cement floor.

I know he's not up there. I can feel it, a howling emptiness that nearly swallows me, but I clatter up the steps anyway.

The loft is just as empty as I imagined, the stubs of candles left unlit on the floor, the blankets on the mattress heaped carelessly against the wall. Danny's colored pencils are strewn all over the floor, half of them broken, amid used sheets of paper.

I'm shaking as I kneel and pick one up. The tree again, slashed dark and angry against the cheap copier paper. It's all there in the pages he left behind—the tree, a flickering candle, the snub nose of Becker's car, my face, my mouth, my hand. And there, at the edge of the pile, his mother, his dad, his brother, Molly, with her round eyes and the same loose curls Danny has.

I drag in a breath, trying to stave it off, but it's too late. I lean over as I vomit all over the papers, a foul splash of dinner and bile. Sweat breaks out on my brow and the back of my neck, slimy and cool, as I wipe my mouth.

He remembers. And he's gone.

It's so chilly I can see my breath as I walk the streets. The shocked, blinking part of my brain imagines a trail of mist superimposed in crazy circles over the neighborhood, a child's scribble on a map.

By just after one my teeth are chattering, and I'm halfway between my street and Danny's. The houses crouch along the streets, folded up for the night like sleeping birds on a wire, window eyes shut. I can't scream for him, and I can't even run after a half hour—I'm too cold and my leg muscles are cramping.

It doesn't usually take so long to walk from my house to Danny's but I'm being careful, walking the blocks in circles, watching for moving shadows. He may have remembered the accident and the night in the graveyard, but there's no guarantee he remembers how to get home, or where exactly home is.

I can't decide if that's a good thing or a bad thing, and it breaks my heart either way.

I'm so panicked, the power inside me is churning in sickening waves. Every time a twig snaps or something moves, I startle, and twice a streak of faint gold light arcs away from me, a sudden flash in the dark. Far down at the end of Dudley, where it turns into Lawrence, the globe in a streetlight explodes, and I have to run when the lights go on in two houses at the sound of shattering glass.

I feel like I could float, fly, so much pure energy is humming through my veins, snaking under my muscles until they're quivering as I walk down each block. It's too much, though, too intense, and when a squirrel runs in front of me on McKinley, a skittering gray shape too close to my feet, I muffle a scream of surprise and watch in horror as it explodes into a cloud of dandelion puffs. The wind carries them away in a starburst, pale green stems wheeling along helplessly.

"Oh my God." I sink to my knees right there on the sidewalk, shaking. I did that. I made a squirrel disappear, change, explode, whatever it was, and I didn't even mean to. *I did that.*

I've done so many things now, and in the big picture one harmless squirrel morphing into a weed isn't exactly tragic, but it doesn't matter. It feels so wrong, as wrong as the cold pallor of Danny's skin under my hands, as wrong as the sickly bright sting of pain in my palm when I sliced it open with the athame.

You're wrong, that voice whispers, cool and slithering in my head. *All wrong.*

I can't stop shaking. I fumble my phone out of my pocket and press the number for Gabriel.

It rings three times before he picks it up, and I cut right through his sleepy, muffled hello.

"He's gone. He's *gone.* I'm walking and I can't find him and I don't know where he is, and what if he does something, Gabriel, he drew all these pictures and—"

"Whoa. *Whoa.* Wren, calm down."

I can't, not right away—the words tumble out of my mouth, broken and breathless, until Gabriel nearly shouts, "Wren, *stop.* Just hold on, okay? I'm on my way."

★ ★ ★

It's after two when Gabriel runs toward me. I stumble straight into his arms and bury my face in his chest, breathing in his heat.

"Hey." He strokes my back briskly as I shiver. "You're frozen."

I am, but it doesn't matter. I shrug off his arms and step back, shaking my head. "We have to find him. Come *on*."

"Wren, you're a Popsicle. Just warm up and tell me everything, all right? Slowly." He bends his head to look me in the eye.

"I told you! He's gone, Gabriel, and we're still blocks from his house and—"

"You're not getting the hang of 'slowly,'" he says, and pulls me back against him. "Put my jacket on at least."

It's got to be near freezing for real now—the grass shimmers with the pale sheen of frost, and the stars are an icy blue. I let him drape the faded army jacket over my shoulders but it's hard not to just bolt, dragging him along behind me. I'm still jittery, echoes of that explosion of power rippling through me, and I can feel time ticking away, every second another chance that someone has seen Danny, paper white and unreal.

No. I swallow back another awful surge of bile.

"Come on," I say, and grab his elbow.

Gabriel blinks in surprise. "*Wait*. Tell me where you've looked, where you think he might be."

"While we walk," I insist, and the wet heat of tears scalds my cheeks. "Come *on*. Are you going to help me or not?"

"Wren," he says, and he's so self-possessed, so logical, talking to me like I'm insane, like he has to be careful or I'll attack at any moment.

He's probably not wrong.

"You need to calm down. I can feel the power in you, and it's like fireworks waiting to be lit." He steps closer slowly, takes the hand I've left outstretched, and closes his fingers around it.

I nod, and wipe the tears away with my free hand. Calm. I can do that.

We're halfway down the block when he glances sideways at me, wincing. "A squirrel, huh?"

He gets an elbow in the ribs in reply, and I don't feel a bit guilty.

"I really thought he would be here."

We're across the street from Danny's house, and it's nearly three now. The sky is slowly losing color, beginning to bleed out the black, but the streets are still sleeping.

The Greers' house is closed up for the night, blinds drawn and doors shut, and in the fading dark it looks sad. As if it's faded in the last few months, too. Even the yard looks shabby in its bare fall clothes.

Gabriel puts his arm around me, but I shrug it off. I know it's wrong—it's the middle of the night and he's here to help me, but standing across the street from Danny's house with another boy's arm around me is wrong, too. Wronger, and I can't even remember if that's a word, but it's still true.

"It's the first place I would have looked," Gabriel says, and if his voice sounds a little strained, I'm not going to apologize. Not right now anyway.

"What if he's inside?" I whisper, squinting across the street. "Or, I don't know, on the back porch?"

"If he was inside, the whole house would be lit up, don't you think?" He glances at me. "I mean, your dead son walks in . . ."

"I know." I rub my temples in exhaustion. I don't want to think about the look on his mother's face if that happens. What would it be? Horror? Relief? Joy? Confusion? All of the above?

"Let's go look, okay?" Gabriel's hand in the small of my back is just enough motivation to get me across the street. We start up the driveway with our heads down, and I don't even know what we're looking for when Gabriel veers left across the dry grass.

I see it then, though. Scuff marks in the grass, as if something has been dragged through it. And then footprints on the porch steps, which stop at the top before turning around again.

"He was here," I whisper, and I glance down the block as if I'll see him walking away.

"He didn't go in," Gabriel says, and he sounds worried. "He went . . . somewhere else. Come on."

He pulls me off the Greers' lawn and down the block to the corner. I'm suddenly so exhausted, I sit down abruptly, landing roughly on the curb. The number of places Danny could have gone seems endless. Becker's, Ryan's, school, even the café . . .

"Let me see," Gabriel says, and grabs my shoulders, shaking me gently until I look up at him.

"See what?"

"Where he might have gone, places that mean something to him," he says, and stares into my eyes.

I try to relax, to open up and picture the places where Danny and I have been together, places where Danny hung out with his friends, anything. I feel the jolt when Gabriel sees the site of the accident. His fingers tighten on my shoulders as the memory of the tree flashes through my mind, the scarred trunk still scorched, pieces of the hood embedded in the bark.

"I can take you there," I say when he lets go. "We have to look everywhere, though. He could have gone to Ryan's house or—"

"No."

I blink. "What do you mean, no? Come on, Gabriel, we can't just sit here. *I* can't just sit here. Whether you want to come or not, I have to find him!"

He takes one hand as I start to stand up, pulling me down again, and I can't shake free. Power pumps through me, urgent and angry, an unfocused hum that needs to be released, but Gabriel says, "Shhh, listen."

I take a deep breath and try to relax, so his voice will cut through that awful buzz.

"It's after three. You need to go home." I shake my head, ready to argue, but he keeps talking, his strong hand clenched firmly around mine. "This is bad, okay? But I can find him, or at least keep looking. I mean, it's going to be bad enough if your mom already figured out you're gone, but if morning rolls around and you're not there?"

A new wave of nausea rolls through me then. *Mom.* I hadn't even thought that far ahead, hadn't thought of anything but finding Danny and getting him back to the loft.

Across the street a dog barks, and I nearly jump out of my skin. In the night silence, it sounds too close, and Gabriel and I stand up at the same time, moving into the shadow of a huge pine. The neighborhood is still asleep, but in the distance on Mountain Avenue I can hear the occasional car passing, and any minute kids with paper routes could start cycling up and down the streets.

"Go home," Gabriel says, and winds his arms around me, pulling me close. "Go home and pretend to get up for school, and when you leave, call me. I'll keep looking."

I want to refuse, tell him it's not his responsibility, that I can handle this on my own, but I can't. I press my cheek to his chest and choke back more stupid, hateful tears. I can't handle this on my own, and I've known it for weeks now.

"I'll make this up to you." The words are muffled into his hoodie, but when I lift my head to kiss him, I know he heard me.

When my alarm goes off at six thirty, I haven't slept for even a minute. I'm so tired I feel sort of drunk, and I'm pretty sure adrenaline is the only reason I can move.

I'm sitting on the edge of my bed when Mom opens my door and sticks her head in, the way she almost always does.

"You up, kiddo?" She's still in the old flannel shirt she wears to bed, and her pillow left a pink crease in one cheek.

"Sort of," I manage to say, and study my bare feet until she closes the door behind her.

I rush through my shower—every time I close my eyes I see the empty loft, the confusion in Danny's eyes when he tells me he can't think, the horrifying image of him walking toward his mother, arms outstretched. . . .

And now it's daylight. Anyone could see him, this marble statue of a boy with dead eyes and cold, gray lips. I throw on jeans and my boots and pull on a ragged black hoodie over a dirty T-shirt, and my hands won't stop shaking. I don't know what's adrenaline and what's the power anymore—there's too much of both, a constant pulsing hum beneath my skin.

My trig book breaks into a pile of dead leaves when I pull it out of my backpack, and when I try to do my hair, it goes purple and blue by turns until I give up. I have to calm down, but if wishing could make it so, I would already be downstairs drinking coffee and pretending I'm heading off for school.

If wishing could make anything so, Danny would be up in the loft and I would be . . . I don't know where. Asleep. In a coma. It sounds pretty good at the moment.

My phone rings just as I'm finally collecting my stuff to head down to the kitchen. I don't bother to look at the display before I flip it open—it has to be Gabriel.

My hello isn't even completely out of my mouth when I hear, "I found him."

CHAPTER SIXTEEN

I'VE NEVER REALLY BEEN NERVOUS ABOUT THE whole meet-the-parents thing. I may dress sort of weird and have a lot of holes in my ears, but I'm little and polite and most of the moms I've met have never even blinked at me hanging out with their kids. Even Danny's mom, who is sort of disgustingly sitcom normal in her sweater sets and khaki pants, loved me.

I'm terrified to meet Gabriel's sister, Olivia, though.

Mostly I'm just plain freaked out to start with, since Gabriel had to walk all the way across town to the park to find Danny, which means Danny had to walk all that way, too.

To the place where he died, and from what Gabriel said on the phone, Danny remembers every minute of it now. Gabriel doesn't want to get too close, and I don't blame him, but he told me he can hear Danny from behind the storage shed where Gabriel's waiting for me. He's sometimes mumbling and sometimes shouting. Stuff about Becker, the car, that night.

Me.

When I stop to think about it, meeting Olivia is actually a lot less scary than seeing Danny is going to be, even though my hand is shaking when I knock on the door to their apartment.

She must have been waiting. The door opens a mere second after I draw my hand away, and the girl standing on the other side looks so much like Gabriel I blink in surprise. She's older, yes, but her hair is the same cool, ashy blond, her eyes only a slightly deeper gray. She's not as tall as he is, but she's taller than I am, and concern has already bled into the tight line of her jaw.

I guess it's better than suspicion.

"I'm Wren," I say needlessly, and she nods.

"Come on in."

Her hair is twisted into a careless knot on top of her head, and she's still in faded sleep pants and a pink YOGA IS LIFE T-shirt. When the door is closed, she leans up against it and folds her arms over her chest.

"You do know how to drive, right?"

In theory is probably the right answer to that question, but Gabriel assured me she doesn't have the same gift he does.

I can't make my mouth work, though, so I simply nod. She considers me for a long minute, her face pinched with worry. She looks kind, pretty cool, but it has to be a little weird to get a phone call from your kid brother at seven fifteen in the morning saying some girl is coming over to borrow your car.

"I don't know," she says finally, and pushes off the door to cross the room toward me. "You look like you're about to jump out of your skin, he sounds like a truck ran over him, and someone needs to tell me what the hell is really going on here."

"I know." It's a cracked whisper, and if she needed any more proof of my nerves, it's right there.

"But he talks about you." Her face softens then, on the way to a smile, and she reaches up to push hair out of my eyes and correct the slant of the green knit cap I pulled on over it. "And I trust him. I have to. He said it would be better if it was just you, so . . ."

I let out a shaky breath when she walks past me and digs into a big brown leather bag, coming up with the keys. She dangles them in front of me and shrugs. "Don't crash it, okay? I hate riding a bike."

I've driven a car—like, actually driven it on a street, not just started it or moved it five feet in the driveway—exactly twice. On a quiet Sunday afternoon early in the summer, and a Tuesday at dinnertime a few days later. Months ago, with my mom in the passenger seat, calmly reminding me to look in the rearview mirror and apply the brakes gently.

It's Friday morning now, one of the busiest times of day in town as everyone heads to school or work. And I have to steer the little blue rust bucket Olivia owns all the way across town, on my own. Just starting the engine is enough to startle me, since the car growls like I kicked it and shudders into gear.

Perfect.

But I can't let myself be nervous. I definitely can't let my power drive me off the road, either, even though it's a close call as I pull into the street and the car practically leaps forward like a bad dog on a leash. The whole thing seems to be vibrating, and I don't know whether that's normal, for this car anyway, or if it's because my head is about to explode with nerves and power.

I don't even turn the radio on as I steer toward town

and then through it, trying not to go too fast or too slow, and once waiting so long at a stop sign that the man in the car behind me lays on his horn. I jolt forward into the intersection and realize I'm chanting, "Just breathe, just breathe," like some demented broken record.

In the end, it takes about nineteen minutes longer than it should have to pull up to the entry to the park, plus two near misses with parked cars, a hellishly confusing traffic circle that actually makes me cry when an old woman in a Subaru gives me the finger, and one time slamming on the brakes so hard I nearly hit my head on the windshield. When I finally get out, I want to drop to the ground and pass out.

But I still have to find Danny, and I pull my phone out to call Gabriel as I break into a run on the wide, paved bicycle path.

"I'm here," I pant as I jog farther into the park. It's empty, too late for most runners and too far away from the playground for moms with little kids. The tree where Becker's car hit is down behind the pond.

"Slow down." Gabriel's voice is tight and low. "He's calm now, but you probably shouldn't startle him. Right now he's sitting against the base of the tree, and I'm behind that shed to your left. Shit, your right. Whichever."

There's only one shed, but Gabriel's beginning to

sound as strung out on exhaustion as I feel, so I just click off the phone and wind down into a fast walk. When I make my way around the sharp bend in the path, the road following along beside me, I notice the tree before I see Danny. It's hard to miss, pointing up like a giant splinter, jagged now at the base.

Danny's sitting with his back against it, but he's facing mostly away from me, looking at the road. His long legs are splayed carelessly in the dirt, and his hands rest on the ground beside them, palms up as if he's waiting to be given something.

An explanation, I think, and shudder a little as I creep through the grass toward the storage shed twenty-five feet away.

Gabriel sags back against the thick vinyl siding when I come around the corner on the far side. "Hey. You in one piece?"

"More or less," I say, and crawl around him to watch Danny, who hasn't moved.

There are a thousand things I could say, probably should say, but as I sit back on my heels and stare at Danny's sculpted, motionless profile, I can't think of any of them. Relief is a hot, thick taste in my mouth, but dread coats it. If I can't think of what to say to Gabriel, I have no idea how to even approach Danny.

But I have to. I have to lead him away from here and into that car and then . . . well, I haven't gotten that far yet, but it doesn't matter. The point is, he can't stay here, even if I'm only now realizing that getting him into Mrs. Petrelli's garage is going to be impossible without being seen. She lives on a busy block with lots of young moms and toddlers who are outside a lot, running around the yards in tiny little jackets while their moms drink coffee on porch steps. I can't risk walking him down my street to cut through the yards, either—I have no idea if Mom would have gone home when she got the call from school that I wasn't there.

"He's been quiet for a while," Gabriel says, so low I have to turn my head to catch it all.

The skin under his eyes looks bruised, and he's lost all the color in his face. I start to trace the curve of one cheekbone with my finger, but pull it back like I've been burned when I remember why we're here, who it is sitting there at the base of that tree. Everything is beginning to feel like it's shifting, moments sliding into one another like watercolors.

"He was still sort of freaked out when I found him," Gabriel whispers. "I don't know how long he'd already been here, though."

I nod, and rock back on my heels before I stand up.

It makes me sick to be scared of facing Danny, when he used to be the safest, best thing in my life. The warm place I could crawl into, the strong hand that was always there to hold mine, the steady pulse in my blood.

The one person I never imagined hurting.

It's broad daylight, and even if it would be more than weird for Danny's mom or Ryan to show up right now, I have to get him out of here. Which means I have to talk to him, look right at the confusion and horror on his face, the familiar, gentle-eyed face that used to do nothing but smile at me. As much as I want to sit here, suspended in the quiet of this chilly, brittle morning, I can't put it off any longer. And it turns out I don't have to.

When I turn my head toward that awful tree, Danny is staring straight at me.

"There was a *crash*."

Danny keeps saying it, and I don't know which one of us he's trying to convince. I'm the one pressed up against the tree now, his hands huge and frighteningly immovable on my shoulders.

Out of the corner of my eye, Gabriel is pacing beside the shed, his hands shaped into useless fists. I told him to stay where he was when I ran toward Danny, who was on his feet and coming toward me faster than I would have thought possible.

I want Danny to deal with me, not Gabriel. And I don't want Gabriel to have to deal with any of this, even if it's a lot too late for that.

"There was." The words sound strangled, but I can't think of anything else to say. There was a crash, and I was so stupid, so unbelievably, insanely stupid to think I could pretend there wasn't.

"A crash, Wren." He shakes me, and I nearly feel Gabriel, just yards away, vibrating with the urge to move. "A car crash."

"I know," I whisper, and turn my face up to him, trying to get him to see me. He's looking right at me, but if I didn't know it was crazy, impossible, I would think he was seeing only the way the road spun out from beneath them, and the broad trunk of the tree looming.

"Wren." He swallows, shakes his head, and for a moment his hands ease up. His eyes are awful, too dark, so glassy they don't seem real. "Wren, did I *die*?"

Oh God.

I wriggle out from under his fingers and wrap my arms around his waist, hanging on.

Hiding my face against his chest.

And really? Just plain hiding.

"Wren." He's not even holding me—his arms are

flung out to his sides as I cling to him, as if he can't bear to touch me now.

It hurts, so much. The sound of his voice, the trembling stiffness in every muscle, so different from the usual cool marble feel of him.

But I can't move. If I let go, what then?

I still don't believe he'll hurt me, not physically. But when I let go, I'll have to look at him again, and truly face what I've done.

Face the fact that he was better off wherever he was before I crept into that cemetery, broken open, pouring all my selfish needs onto his grave.

He had to be. I don't know what I believe about God or heaven or even hell, but if there is a heaven, I know Danny was there. He was nothing but good, a teenage boy who kissed his mom before he left for school in the morning and drew funny pictures for his girlfriend's little sister, just to make her laugh.

A boy who gave his girlfriend everything he had, freely. Slow-curving grins in the halls between class, long hand-in-hand walks on windy afternoons, a voice in the dark when something hurt, ridiculous, awesome dreams about rock stardom and comic-book superheroes. His kisses, his hands, his long legs, a whole new world to map out, together.

And what did I give him? A half-life in the loft of a musty garage, and a girl who didn't even think about who it might hurt before she reached out and grabbed what she wanted.

"Wren." He insinuates his fingers between his body and my arms, peeling me away from him with a grunt. "Did I *die*? Did I?"

I stumble when he pushes me, not hard, but enough to back me into the unforgiving bulk of the tree. It's a lot less than I deserve, but I still have to hold up a hand to keep Gabriel from charging toward us.

He's inched closer, maybe only a dozen feet away now, but when Danny sees him it doesn't seem to register. Gabriel, a stranger, has no part in this for him—it's all me, me and the memories that cloud his eyes.

I straighten up, trying to catch my breath. My heart is pounding, and the shocking rush of adrenaline is nothing compared to the hot, violent buzz of power beneath my skin. It needs to go somewhere, and it's hard to contain it now—fear and guilt and grief are feeding it, making it more and more potent.

"Wren, tell me!" Danny shouts, pushing his hands through his hair. He's wheeling now, staggering circles in the dying autumn grass. "Did I *die*? What is this? I remember it, Wren! We . . . we *crashed*. Becker was . . .

There was the radio, and I thought . . . And you, Wren, I was thinking, I kept thinking, and then . . ."

I know I'm crying as he goes on like that, I can feel the wet heat on my cheeks in the chill of the morning, but I can't do anything about it. I can't move, I can't speak, I can't do anything but watch as Danny remembers.

There's nothing left inside me but a single word, *stop*, and it echoes like an alarm. *Stop, stop, stop*, endless, because that's where this has been heading all along.

I have to stop. Danny has to stop. Everything needs to stop until I make this right.

I don't even move when Danny turns and finally sees me again, the storm of memories clearing and simple horror replacing them. For a moment that seems as fragile and weightless as a soap bubble, he just stares as I stand there, my hands clenched, tears streaming.

Then he charges.

I can hear Gabriel's feet on the dry grass, thudding closer, but it's too late for him to do anything. It's all up to me now, again.

I've never done this before, not even when I needed Danny to go to sleep. Then it was just words, a suggestion fed to him with nothing more than the sound of my voice, the gentle sweep of my hands on his back.

That's not going to work this time.

So I focus everything inside me on that single word, and push it at Danny with the force of all my power behind me: *"Stop!"*

The air around us crackles, blue-green with ozone, and he snaps like his strings have been cut, falling three feet away from me in a twisted jumble of arms and legs and too-long hair.

Even Gabriel's not quick enough to catch me when I fall, too.

CHAPTER SEVENTEEN

WHATEVER I DID HIT ME NEARLY AS HARD AS Danny, and I can barely see through the throbbing howl of pain in my head as Gabriel drives us back to his place. When I look at Danny slumped in the backseat, my stomach joins the protest, and I have to point my face at the cold air streaming through the open window so I won't puke.

I open my eyes when the car stops in the driveway behind the big old Victorian where Gabriel and Olivia's apartment is. I can't believe we have to bring him here.

Not in the condition he's in right now, anyway.

He looks, more than ever, dead. He's so pale he

practically gleams in the crisp autumn sunlight, and the cool blue veins in his hands and arms stand out like the tracings on a map.

"You're going to have to help me with the doors and stuff," Gabriel says, getting out of the car and handing me the keys. He's pale, too, drawn into himself like a turtle, and I can't do more than nod when I get out and join him on the other side of the car.

It's just as awkward and horrible getting Danny out of the car as it was getting him into it, one limp arm lolling out to smack the open door, his head just missing the roof. Gabriel's tall, but he's lean, and Danny is just as big—maneuvering him up over Gabriel's shoulder would be funny if Danny were drunk, maybe, but now? It's awful, just another reminder that the boy Gabriel's lugging into the house and up the stairs is dead.

Olivia opens the door to the apartment before I can even get the keys out. "I heard the car," she says, and steps back as Gabriel struggles over the threshold and heads straight for his room.

Which leaves me face-to-face with Olivia, who is clearly a little freaked out by the kid draped over her brother's shoulder.

"Is he okay?" she says, craning her head to watch as Gabriel sort of dumps Danny on his bed.

"Not so much." And wow, that's the understatement of the millennium, but I'm so exhausted and in so much pain, it's amazing I can get my mouth to form words.

In my pocket, my phone buzzes again—it's been going off pretty steadily for the last half hour. I know it's my mom, that school must have called when I didn't show up for homeroom, but there's no way I can even think about answering it now.

There's no way I can think, period. My brain is idling rougher and rougher, ready to sputter out and die, and as I stand there with Olivia frowning at me, I realize my stomach is going to backfire first.

I'm not sure where the bathroom is, but I bolt in the direction of the bedrooms and see a door standing open to reveal old white tile and an even older pedestal sink. I make it that far and lean over, retching up I don't even know what. I can't remember the last time I ate.

I'm mostly done when I feel a light hand on my shoulder, and lift my head to find Olivia there. She brushes the sweaty feathers of my bangs off my forehead and flips down the lid on the toilet so I can sit. I'm vibrating like a plucked guitar string, and my head is still screaming at me, hot red fury.

I close my eyes, even though I can hear Gabriel's footsteps, the creak of the door as he leans against it.

The water's running, and the next thing I know a cool washcloth is gently passed over my forehead and my cheeks. Olivia picks up my hands and runs the cloth over each wrist, and it feels so good, I sigh out loud.

"You need to lie down, kiddo." Olivia gently tilts my head forward and presses the washcloth to the back of my neck. "Think you can stand up?"

I open my eyes and nod, and Gabriel steps out of the way when Olivia helps me to my feet and steers me toward the door. My phone buzzes again, and as I collapse onto the sofa I pull it out and toss it across the room. It lands somewhere with a plastic thud, and Olivia winces.

"Can you give us a minute?" Gabriel says quietly, and I study the dirty knees of my jeans so I don't have to see the look I know is probably passing between them.

"I need to know the whole story here at some point, guys," Olivia says, and although her voice is sharp, her hand in my hair is as gentle as it was in the bathroom. "I'm guessing we don't need nine-one-one for the kid in your room?"

"No." It's little more than a croak, but it's the best I can do.

Gabriel sits down next to me. After a silent moment that stretches so thin I can almost hear it snapping, Olivia nods and goes into her bedroom, shutting the door behind her.

"I can't," I say when she's gone, and Gabriel's reaching out to put his arms around me. I'm still trembling, and even holding my head up is an effort. There's no power humming inside me now, just the stale backwash of adrenaline and fear and exhaustion. "Not right now."

Somewhere across the room my phone buzzes again, and Gabriel gets up. "I'll put that on silent, okay?"

I'm not sure if I even nod. I'm out before my head hits the arm of the sofa, and for once I don't even dream.

There's a warm, heavy weight against my thigh when I open my eyes, and I struggle up on my elbows to find that it's Gabriel's head. He's on the floor beside the sofa, and in sleep his head has rolled back against my leg.

The temptation to run my fingers through that fine, sandy hair is almost overwhelming, before I'm fully awake and everything comes rushing back.

It hits me like a slap in the face, and I blink as I sit up and look for a clock. There isn't one, but Gabriel's phone is lying on the floor next to him. I have to reach around him to pick it up, and he stirs as I do.

"Hey," he says, rubbing his eyes as I squint at the screen of his phone. Two o'clock. Mom must be frantic.

I think I sort of grunt at Gabriel in reply, because suddenly all I can think about is finding my phone, listening to the messages I know must be on there, and figuring out what the hell to do next. And that's before even considering Danny, who I hope is still in Gabriel's room.

If he's not, I don't want to think about what will happen next.

My left leg is asleep, and I wince as I set it down, pins and needles prickling hot. My head doesn't hurt anymore, but I'm still vaguely nauseous, hollowed out. Gabriel catches hold of my hand before I try to stand.

"I'll get your phone," he says, "and something for you to drink. Just stay here for a second."

I won't cry again—there can't be any tears left anyway. But the kindness in Gabriel's eyes is so sweet, and so undeserved, I have to look away when he lets go of me to walk into the kitchen.

But I can't sit still, either, and my leg isn't numb anymore, so I get up and follow him. The kitchen overlooks the backyard, and the car is gone so I assume Olivia is, too.

Gabriel takes a bottle of water out of the fridge and hands it to me before pointing to my phone, which is lying on the table. He doesn't seem completely awake yet, and it's so quiet in the apartment, I simply nod.

I glance at the closed door where Danny is before I take my phone back out to the living room and settle on the sofa. At some point I'm going to have to go in there, and the fact that I would rather listen to the angry messages on my phone instead makes me queasy all over again.

There are four phone messages, and six texts, which is actually less than I expected. Mom's first message is tentative and a little confused: "Wren? Were you late? School called and said you missed homeroom. Everything okay?"

Her next two messages aren't as pleasant, and the one from Jess is short but effective: "Where the hell are you, Wren?"

The texts are all from Jess but one, which is from Dar, and it simply reads: WREN? It's just the one word, but I can picture her face as she typed it, hair falling into her face, a confused frown twisting her mouth.

I'm so very screwed. On every level, in every way. In ways they haven't invented yet, actually. It's tempting to throw my phone across the room again, get up and walk out of the apartment, and just . . . keep going. Walk until I can't walk anymore, until I reach the edge of the world, or at least the edge of town.

Like a coward. God, that voice never shuts up. It's

always there, always ready to point out every horrible, stupid thing I want to ignore. If it's my conscience, it's working overtime, not that anyone asked it to.

I'm still slumped on the sofa, my phone in my hands, when Gabriel comes into the room and sits next to me. For a minute, he's as still as Danny, but then I feel his hand on the back of my neck, a steady weight. It's even more tempting to lean back into it, let him catch me, but I can't. I won't.

The pressure of Gabriel's hand changes, and I finally turn my head to face him. I can see the things he's considering saying, as if the words were scrolling past.

"Don't say it's going to be okay."

His smile is small and sad, and I feel a little guilty for being so cold. "I wasn't. It's not. But you're going to get through it. And I can help you, Wren. I will help you, I promise."

"Why?" I push up off the sofa and cross the room, arms folded over my chest, trying to hold in all the things I want to say, should say. "This is so not your problem."

"You know why."

"Then you must be as crazy as I am," I say, and the words are bitten off, jagged and ugly in the silence. "Why would you want to be with me? After . . . after all of *this*?"

"Nothing's that black and white, Wren." When he looks up at me, his eyes are stormy, a deep cloudy gray. "You know that."

"What I know is I have to go home and try to explain to my mother where I was today, and then try to make Jess and Dar forgive me for ruining tonight, and *then* figure out how to . . ." I choke on the words I need to finish the sentence, but Gabriel follows my gaze to the closed door of his room, and I think he knows what I mean anyway. "God, how am I going to get him back to the loft?"

"What are you talking about?" Now he's on his feet, and he's looking at me like I've really lost my mind. "We decided to bring him here."

"For *now*," I say helplessly. "While it was daylight. He can't stay here!"

"Why not?" For someone who's being completely oblivious, he's still looking at me like I'm the crazy one.

"Oh yeah, Olivia will love that." I pull out my best sneer, the one that's gotten me into trouble with teachers too many times to count. "I can see it now, you'll be all sensible and calm, 'Olivia, there's this epically whacked girl I like, and we need to keep her dead boyfriend here for a while, okay?' That'll go over great. Let me know when she signs you up for therapy and the good drugs."

"She already knows."

My mouth falls open. "What?"

"She already knows. We talked while you were asleep, before she left for work."

My heart skips a beat, a frightening moment of nothing where it seems suspended in my chest, open and gasping.

"Gabriel, what exactly did you tell her?"

He comes closer, and takes one of my hands. "The truth." He shrugs.

"The truth." My voice sounds faint, and I can't come up with anything else to say. I assumed she would think Danny was on drugs or something, which was bad enough, but the truth?

I'm still gaping when Gabriel squeezes my hand. "Look, I know it's weird, but there are things I haven't told you either. It's not something either of us have seen before, obviously, but just trust me, okay? It's cool."

"How is it cool, Gabriel?" I wrench my hand away. "And what do you mean things you've never told me?" My heart's beating fine again, but now I feel smothered, like there's not enough air in the room. This isn't his problem, and now his sister knows about me, knows what I did to Danny, what Danny is, and if I ever thought I could keep my life from getting completely snarled with

Gabriel's when this is over, I was so wrong.

"Stop that." He follows as I back up against the wall, breathing hard to make sure I keep breathing at all. He stops just short of me, though, and holds up his hands. I can feel him in my head, just a gentle pressure, and I close my eyes.

"No fair."

"I'm sorry." He waits until I open my eyes again. He's still, but his face is set hard, resolute. "It's not like that, I swear. I want to help, Wren. And you can't take him back to that garage. He left once, and you know he's not going to be content to stick around anymore, not unless you can pull some more magic out of your hat."

Shit. He's right, of course he's right, and I hate it.

"Don't . . . don't look in my head," and I know I sound sullen, all of five years old, but I have to remind him that there are boundaries, even if I can't remember to keep within them all the time.

"I'm sorry."

When he reaches for my hand this time, I let him take it. Despite how Danny scared me in the park, I hate the idea of him not being right there, only the length of my backyard away from me. "This is just for now, though. I'm going to figure this out."

"Right." There's nothing hidden in his eyes now,

and I can't help but believe him. "It's the weekend as of tonight. If nothing else, I'll be here when Olivia isn't."

"Yeah." I glance at his bedroom door again, amazed that it's still quiet inside.

"Just go," Gabriel says softly, and his thumb runs over the back of my hand. "Deal with your mom and everything. I'll call you if . . . well, I'll call you later."

I don't put up a fight when he kisses my forehead, a whisper of pressure. But it seems important that I'm the one to let go of his hand first.

CHAPTER EIGHTEEN

MOM'S CAR IS IN THE DRIVEWAY WHEN I GET home, and that's such a bad thing. She only leaves the salon during the day if dragons have attacked or it's raining grape juice, so she's clearly counting this as a disaster. It's not like I didn't expect it—I've never skipped before, not a whole day anyway.

I'm probably only imagining the dark smudge of cloud hanging specifically over our house.

I don't bother to be quiet when I shut the front door behind me, and I leave my backpack in a heap on the floor beneath the coatrack. A chair scrapes across the kitchen floor, and Mom's standing in the doorway to the kitchen a second later.

"Well, you're not dead," she says tightly. Her hair, usually pulled up into a neat knot at the back of her head, has escaped half its pins, and her eyes are bruised with worry. "Or hurt. You may wish you were in a minute, though."

I swallow hard and stand my ground.

"Care to explain?" She leans against the doorjamb, arms folded over her chest. It's all too casual—I know her, and I know she's seething inside.

"I cut school." I should have thought of a reason to give her when I was walking home, but I was too busy freaking out about what might happen if Danny comes out of his magic coma.

"That's pretty clear, Wren." She takes a step forward, and I can feel her power lashing now, crackles of electricity in the air around her. She's usually better at keeping it hidden, controlling it, and I'm suddenly scared by the fact that she's not even trying this time. "Why?"

This is the hard part. I don't want to tell her about Gabriel, not now, maybe not for a while. And even if I did, I wouldn't want the first thing she heard to be that I cut school with him for the day. Do I lie and say Jess and Darcia and I all ditched together, with the sleepover planned for tonight? Would she even believe that Dar would skip school for the day? Jess is a no-brainer, but Dar follows rules like her life depends on it.

"I called Jess and Darcia," Mom says while I'm still scrambling, trying to come up with a believable story. "So if you're thinking of adding them to whatever lie you're working on, don't bother."

I lift my chin. Fine. There's no reason to drag anyone else into this when I'm the one who deserves all the blame.

"I'm not going to lie," I say, and I'm proud that my voice isn't even shaking. Every other part of me is, though, whether Mom can see it or not. "I was . . . in a bad mood. I skipped. That's it."

"That's it." She lifts a brow. "And you couldn't bother to return even one of my calls."

"I was skipping school, Mom." Inside, my own power is humming to life, a buzz of exhaustion and frustration. Why can't she just punish me and get it over with? "I wasn't exactly in the mood to chat."

She actually snorts, and takes another step closer. "But you thought letting me worry all day was better than admitting that you'd cut? You really thought I'd be angrier about you missing one day of school than having to wonder all day if you'd been hit by a car or decided to run away?"

"Mom . . ."

"Don't!" The word is followed by a single brief shudder of power, and the air ripples around us. She ignores it, just like always. "Haven't we talked about telling the truth, Wren? What happened to honesty?"

That's it—I'm too tired and too shattered to fight it anymore.

"Yeah, Mom, what about honesty?" I know I'm shaking visibly now, and I can't help the pulse of power that slips free, rattling the windows and the framed pictures on the wall. "What about you being honest with me for a change?"

She looks like she's been slapped. And when she doesn't say anything, I just shake my head. I knew it.

I pound up the stairs and slam the door to my room so hard, it feels like the whole world vibrates.

Neither Jess nor Darcia will answer my calls, even after school is out for the day. I text them both, nothing more than I'M SO SORRY and LET ME EXPLAIN, but I know it's too late. Tonight was supposed to be our big reunion, a return to the days when a sleepover at one house or another was a given on any weekend, when we shared everything and never thought any of us would want it any other way.

Now it's too hard. Now I would have to admit to them what I did to Danny, and I can't even think about the look on their faces if they knew the truth.

Right now, as much as I hate the whole idea of whatever I'm facing, it's better than worrying about anything else. If I let myself linger on the image of Danny banging down the door to Gabriel's room—or banging down *Gabriel*—my stomach rolls and heaves like a wild sea. And if I let myself remember Mom talking about honesty, the hum just beneath my skin roars to life, buzzing hot and furious. Looking through the dusty books I've dragged out from the depths of my closet is almost a relief, even if I'm researching a way to accomplish the most horrible thing I can imagine.

I'm not surprised that Mom didn't follow me up the stairs, since talking about what we are is always the last thing she wants to do. When the door opens now, I shove the spell book I'm reading under the bed and brace myself, but it's not her, it's Robin.

She's drawn in on herself the way she does when Mom and I fight, hair hanging in her face, her mouth pinched. She doesn't wait for an invitation, but plops down on the bed next to me, and immediately grunts.

"God, Wren, what's under here?" She moves and starts to flip back the comforter, where the rest of the books are hidden, and I snatch them up before she can get a decent look. I hope.

"Oh, like your room is such a model of cleanliness," I say, and shove the books into the bottom drawer of my desk. "What's up, kid?"

"Don't call me that," she mutters, but she doesn't get up and leave in a huff the way she usually does. Instead, she picks at a loose strand on the hem of her sweater and folds her legs under her as if she's settling in.

I want to scream her out of the room, but I can't. As annoying as she can be, Robin is my little sister, and she looks as lost and confused as I've ever seen her.

"What's wrong?" I sit down beside her and pull her hair off her forehead, scraping it back with my fingers shaped into a loose comb.

"You tell me." Her eyes are so honest, everything she feels right there for me to see. "Mom's . . . being weird. Like, weirder than usual."

"What do you mean?"

"She was burning leaves in the backyard. Without matches. And it was all blue and purple and green."

Shit.

"She stopped when I went back there, but Wren . . ." Robin shakes her head, and the first hint of tears makes her eyes gleam wet and bright. "I don't get it. I mean, she won't explain it, and you won't explain it, and now I'm starting to . . ."

Shit. I put my arm around her and pull her closer, and I can feel the power in both of us—my fury, her frustration, twined and humming hard.

"I know," I tell her, useless and helpless and so angry at my mother and myself, I could cry with her if it wouldn't be so much more satisfying to scream instead.

I've held tight to my memories of Dad, big and warm and smiling as he tucked me into bed or hoisted me onto his shoulders. And I've never let myself forget when Aunt Mari and Gram were regular fixtures in the house. Aunt Mari was always around, usually laughing with Mom, and Gram was outside with me a lot, watching me play or bent over the flower beds, coaxing tulips and daffodils open. Everything Gram planted has died since then.

So many of those memories are just fluttering scraps I have to grab at now: Aunt Mari singing to baby Robin, trailing a hand in the air so streaks of glittery color danced to the melody. Gram bending over a pot on the stove, waving the flame higher so good smells floated into the kitchen. The three of them, Mom, Mari, and Gram, sitting around the dining room table looking at old photos, some hanging precariously in midair so everyone could see them. Dad always nearby, smiling, not exactly part of it, but content to watch.

But Robin doesn't remember any of that. I don't know if it's worse that she doesn't, or that I *do*, that I know there was a time when our power wasn't something Mom denied, and Aunt Mari and our grandmother were still a part of our lives. What I don't know is why that changed.

"I know it's starting for you," I finally say, still holding her, pressing the words into the tangled silk of her hair. "And it's not a bad thing. It's not, no matter how Mom acts. But there are . . . rules to it."

"How are we supposed to know what they are if Mom won't tell us?" Robin protests, and pushes away so she can look me in the eye. "I know you can do things, I've seen you, and you don't care if Mom doesn't want you to."

I'm older than you is a lame thing to say, and so is pretty much everything else I can think of, especially when she's staring at me, confused and defiant and afraid all at once. Especially when right now it feels like I would have been better off never testing the energy inside me.

"You have to know how to use it, Robin," I say instead. It's weak and I hate it, because Mom could teach us both, could explain what it means and how to control it, but I'm not going to be the one to tell my little sister to start experimenting, not when my dead boyfriend is just a few blocks away.

"But Mom could teach us!" She gets up and kicks one of my Chucks across the floor. It slides into a pile of dirty clothes and she stares at it, arms folded. She's attempting sullen, but I know she's trying not to cry. "And I know you guys were fighting because of it. Neither of you tell me anything."

"We weren't, Binny," I say softly. It's almost true, anyway. "Not today."

"Whatever." She shakes her hair over her shoulders and faces me, mouth set tight. "I'm just sick of it. I come home and find her making, like, magical rainbow fire in the backyard and I'm just supposed to pretend that—"

The door swings open, cutting her off. Mom looks calm enough now, but I know she's just trying to smooth things over for Robin.

"I need to talk to your sister, Robin."

"I figured." Robin pushes past her, and on any other day Mom would scold her for being rude. "I'll be downstairs if anyone wants to keep some more stuff from me."

I brace myself, but Mom doesn't even bat an eyelash, and we stare at each other while Robin pounds down the stairs.

CHAPTER NINETEEN

I BREAK BEFORE MOM DOES. BIG SURPRISE. SHE could outstare a Zen master.

"So, am I grounded? No TV, no phone? What?"

"Don't start with me, Wren. I'm too angry."

I shrug. "Start what? There are consequences, I get that. I just want to know what they are."

Mom comes all the way into the room and shuts the door behind her. It's not quite loud enough for a slam, but since she did it without touching the door, I get the message.

"You really think it's as simple as that? You cut school, I punish you, it's all over?"

I lift my chin and sit up straighter. "Why not? What else is there?"

It's dangerous to provoke her, especially right now, but in my head, so much of this is her fault. Even though in my heart I know that's a lie, I want someone to blame, someone I can shout at, someone who's not me.

"Where were you today, Wren?" She's bristling, her power practically shimmering around her in jagged sparks.

"God, why do you care?" I fling the words at her as if they'll actually break skin, draw blood. "Because I won't tell you? Because I'm keeping a secret? What about your secrets, Mom? What about all the things you won't tell me?"

It feels good to shout, to open the door and let everything out, the way it did when I realized Gabriel knew what I was.

"That's not the issue here," Mom says, and her voice is too calm, too steady. I can see her holding back, and I hate it. If I'm going to lose it, I want her to lose it, too. More than that, I want her to tell me the truth for once.

"No? Well, I'm not dead and I'm not pregnant and I'm not on drugs, so you've got nothing to worry about, okay?" I fold my arms across my chest and stare up at her. Her eyes flash hot and angry. "You've got your secrets, I've got mine."

"Stop." The room crackles and flares bright with lightning, but it's not lightning, it's her, and I have to hold myself steady to keep from shrinking back against the pillows.

"Why, Mom? Because I'm actually being honest now?" I know Robin must be able to hear us—hell, the whole neighborhood can probably hear us—but I don't care about that.

"You don't understand, Wren." The room is still pulsing with the last shudder of her outburst, as if her heartbeat is echoing in the air and the walls. "You don't know anything about it."

"So tell me! Tell us!" I shake my head. She doesn't have any idea how wrong she is. "I can *do* things, Mom. So can Robin! Did you think we weren't going to notice?"

"Wren," Mom begins in a warning tone, holding up a hand, but I ignore it.

"No!" I'm on my feet now, and practically screaming, but it feels right, the words pouring out with the tears now hot and wet on my face. "Forget it, Mom. I'm done. I'm done pretending, I'm done ignoring the stuff you don't want to explain. This is part of me, part of us, our whole family, and we don't even have that anymore. You don't talk to Aunt Mari and Gram is dead and Dad is gone, and I know it has something to do with . . . this." I wave my arms as if taking it all in, and let the energy surging inside me flash out in ripples of soundless vibrations that rattle the windows.

"You don't know anything about that," Mom says, stepping closer, and she's crying too now. "You don't know. . . ."

Whatever it is, she can't bring herself to finish the sentence, and I shake my head.

"Well, I'm asking you to tell me," I say, wiping my cheeks with the back of my hand. "This is my life, too, Mom! My life, me, and you act like this huge thing is just . . . nothing. I'm done. *Done.*"

I snatch my backpack off the bed before she can react, and I'm long gone by the time thunder claps overhead and it starts to pour.

There's only one place to go, and Gabriel opens the door to the apartment looking as drained and broken as I feel.

"What's wrong?" I ask right away, but he just stands back so I can see into the living room.

Where Danny is pacing, a pale column of a boy, holding himself stiff as he walks back and forth from the window to the far wall. He's muttering, even though I can't make out what he's saying.

When he turns around, he sees me and his face changes immediately. It's not joy like it used to be, but at least he doesn't look ready to strangle me, either.

"Wren."

I swallow back my nerves and walk into the room as Gabriel shuts the door. I'm so not ready for this, not after what just happened with Mom, but it's not like I have a choice. And I want to know what happened, how he woke up, how Gabriel has kept him calm.

"You were gone," Danny says when I'm within arm's reach, and takes me by the shoulders to pull me against him.

I'd almost forgotten how cold he is after the warm press of Gabriel's mouth.

"I came back," I whisper against the chilly fabric of his T-shirt. It's dirty now, smeared with dust and the broken remains of leaves, and I wonder exactly what happened during that long walk from the loft to his house and then to the park.

"Wren, I was dead." He's whispering, too, as if Gabriel shouldn't hear us, and I venture a glance at him, to make sure he's still in the room.

I don't think anything's ever hurt more than being afraid of Danny. I'm not sure anything ever will.

"I know," I say, and push away just enough to take his hand and lead him to the sofa. "I know."

He sits without protest, but he doesn't let go of my hand, so I wind up beside him, nearly in his lap. He's all bones, pale and hard, but his eyes are gleaming again, too dark.

"I'm . . . I was dead, Wren. I remember."

"I know. I'm sorry." I wince when his fingers tighten around my hand.

"And now?" He leans closer, and I try not to shiver. "What am I now, Wren? What did you *do*?"

It sounds so much like Gabriel, the day he figured it out. But worse. So much worse. It's like Danny knows what I did and he can't make himself admit it.

Can't make himself believe that I would bring him back, or give him this awful shadow life.

I lay my hand on his leg. "Danny, it's going to be okay." Wow, there's the biggest lie I've ever told, and it sounds so weak, so ridiculous, even I wouldn't believe it.

"Wren, I remember," he says again, still leaning close. "I . . . remembered before, but I didn't know . . . all I wanted was you, before."

And now it's not enough. It was never going to be enough, of course, and I don't know why I couldn't understand that when I chanted the words that would bring him back to me.

To me, for me, only me. I was so selfish.

It doesn't seem possible, but I'm crying again, slow tears that roll down my cheeks and splash onto my shirt. "I'm sorry," I whisper, because I don't know what else to say.

Gabriel speaks instead, and even Danny looks up at the sound of his voice.

"But you love Wren, right, Danny? You love her more than anything?"

It sounds cruel, throwing that back at him, but oddly it seems to satisfy Danny. He sits back a little, relaxing, and he nods. "I do. I do love you, Wren."

My voice is broken when I whisper, "I love you, too."

I want to say more, to reassure him somehow that I'll fix this, but before I can think of anything that's not a complete lie, Gabriel comes a little closer.

"What did you tell me, about the first time you met? That you thought she was weird, but also weirdly pretty?"

My head snaps up in alarm, but Danny is smiling now, and his gaze is focused on something far away.

"She was," he says absently. "She is. Like a little bird, because her hair was like feathers, and then she told me her name and I thought she was kidding."

I remember that, and suddenly the moment is so clear

it's like it happened only a second ago. I glance at Gabriel, but he's concentrating on Danny, leaning forward to encourage him to tell more of the story. When he sees me looking, he adds, "Danny's been telling me all about you. How you met and where, the things you used to do together. All the reasons he loves you."

And I get it then—he's been focusing on Danny's best memories, of me anyway, to keep him talking, to keep him calm. To keep him from remembering that he can't go home, can't see his mother or his friends, because he was supposed to be dead and buried months ago.

It's surreal, the two of them, light and dark, tall and taller, two boys who shouldn't have anything to say to each other, sitting in the same room and talking about me. For a moment, I close my eyes and press my fingers into them, hard, until streaky light explodes behind my closed lids. My life cannot get any more insane.

"I love Wren," Danny repeats, but this time he sounds as if he needs to be convinced. He looks at me, dark eyes huge and flat, and then at Gabriel, and his brow pulls up into a frown. "Wren?"

"Did you tell him about the comic strip?" I say quickly.

It's the first thing that comes to mind, and something he loves, but he's not going to be distracted now. He shifts on the sofa, grabbing my hand again, and I wince at the strength of his grip.

"Wren?"

The unspoken question is clear—who is this guy? Danny was never the jealous type, not that he had any reason to be, but this isn't really Danny, not anymore. And the part of the boy I loved that's still in there is confused and betrayed and horrified already.

Gabriel is still, tense, and I can't tell if he's ready to bolt or jump at Danny. I don't want either to happen, so instead I carefully tug at Danny's hand, pulling him to his feet as I stand up.

"Why don't we go in the bedroom and talk alone?" My heart stutters awkwardly in my chest, but only because I'm planning to do all the talking, and I'm already scrambling for the right words.

For a moment, he doesn't move, and his gaze is trained on Gabriel. It's as if he just realized the kid talking to him all this time must have some connection to me, and the expression on his face is beginning to frighten me. "Danny." I concentrate, throwing a little of my power behind the word, and it hums in the silence, a vibrating echo, until he swings his eyes toward me. His face softens, just enough, and I pull him into Gabriel's bedroom while he's cooperative.

It's stupid, but my first thought when I shut the door behind us is that I'm seeing Gabriel's room for the first time without Gabriel. With, in fact, another boy. A boy I still love.

Rooms are important, I think—or maybe I'm just a snoop. But they've always fascinated me, the things you see in someone's bedroom that you might not have expected. The huge poster of a shirtless Taylor Lautner in Darcia's bedroom, for instance. The book on financial freedom for women beside Aunt Mari's bed.

But there's no time to think about the lack of things in Gabriel's room, which is the most startling aspect of it. Instead of a secret teddy bear or, like, appalling boy band CDs, there's almost nothing but his clothes, a dresser, and his bed.

And the bed is where Danny pulls me right away, sitting down abruptly and pulling me after him. I don't try to wrestle away—my power was always stronger when we were touching. I think back then it was just love, sheer happiness bubbling out, the same way my power pushes restlessly at me when I'm angry or upset.

Now, who knows? I'm feeling all of those things anyway.

"Wren, I want—"

I cut him off with a finger pressed to his lips. "Shhh."

He blinks once, waiting, and I gather everything inside me, sweeping it all into my center where I can feel it grow into a deep pulse of power. *Sleep,* I think, focusing the unspoken word at him. *Sleep easy. I'll wake you. Sleep until then. Sleep easy.*

I've never done anything like this before, not without speaking aloud, but it seems to work. After a moment, he blinks again, sleepy-eyed now, and his arms begin to relax. In another minute he's slumping, and I catch him before he falls like a mannequin onto the bed.

Once he's down, he doesn't move, even when I slide carefully off the mattress. I know he doesn't feel the cold, that he's not even really asleep, but I can't help myself—I glance around until I find a big bath sheet on the floor that I can gently drape over him before I leave.

Gabriel walks out of the kitchen when I shut the door to his bedroom.

"Okay?"

I nod, even though it's really not.

"You look like you've been awake for about a month," he says, and brushes hair off my forehead.

"I hope you don't say that to all the girls," I say a little weakly, but I manage a smile. He doesn't look much better, and when I glance at the clock it's only six. I have no idea where to go, what to do, and all I can think of is passing out for the next week or so, and hoping to wake up and discover it was all a really bad dream.

"I made tea," Gabriel says, and walks back to the kitchen to get a mug. It's still steaming, and I carry it into the living room. It's dark already, and without the lights on the room feels like a hiding place, safe and quiet and private.

I curl up on one end of the couch and balance the mug on my knee, letting the warmth bleed through to my hands. When Gabriel goes to turn on the one lamp, I say, "Don't."

He doesn't question me. Instead, he comes to sit beside me, and looks at me for a minute before he pulls my feet up and starts to unlace my boots. They fall to the floor, two heavy thuds, and then it's silent again.

There's too much to talk about, so we don't talk at all. But I'm grateful to have someone to sit with me in the dark.

CHAPTER TWENTY

WAKING UP ON GABRIEL'S SOFA IS STARTING TO feel weirdly familiar, which is something I definitely would not have guessed a week ago. My neck is stiff and my right foot is asleep, but I push into a sitting position as quietly as I can, because Gabriel is still out on the other end of the couch.

And Olivia is sitting on the coffee table, drinking what smells like strong coffee and smiling at me sort of sheepishly. "Hey," she says.

I blink and swallow. The inside of my mouth feels like a sweaty sock, and I'm uncomfortably aware of the way my hair is sticking up in seventeen directions. "Um. Hey."

"There's a spare toothbrush in the bathroom, if you want." She smiles over her mug and glances at Gabriel. "He'll probably be out for a while still. But there's coffee and breakfast, too. You must be starving."

I am, I realize as my stomach responds with a painful twist. I can't remember the last time I ate anything substantial, and we must have fallen asleep crazy early. The last thing I remember is putting down my mug of tea and letting Gabriel gather me against him so I could tuck my head into his shoulder.

And Olivia must have come home and found us together. My cheeks heat suddenly, but she's already getting up, calling softly over her shoulder, "There are doughnuts in the kitchen. But you'll have to fight me for the last chocolate one."

When it comes to cool, Olivia definitely takes the gold. By the time I finally make my way into the kitchen, my hair sort of tamed and my teeth brushed, she has a huge mug of coffee poured for me and the doughnuts arranged on a plate. I pull out the stool at the breakfast bar and climb onto it, not sure what to say.

She takes care of that, too, though. "So," she says, topping off her coffee before leaning on the counter across from me. "How are you holding up?"

I blow across my mug and shrug. "Not at complete

meltdown yet? But pretty close."

"I figured." She takes a deep breath and straightens up. "Gabriel told me most of it, and I sort of filled in the rest. Was he your first?"

I blink at her. "My . . . first?"

"Love," she says, and her smile is a little sad. "Danny, I mean."

Oh. I nod, and stare into my cup again, hoping the color on my cheeks isn't too obvious.

"It's a big deal. Don't let anyone tell you different. Not that . . . well, you know."

I meet her eyes again. "I do know. Now, anyway. I just . . . I didn't even feel like I could breathe without him. I know that's stupid."

"It's not stupid at all." She swallows the last of her coffee and sets down her mug, tilting her head before she speaks again. "Most people would want exactly what you wanted in the same situation, and most people wouldn't understand that it could never work, either. It's just that most of us can't do what you can."

"I know."

"I don't want to go all Spiderman here, but 'with great power comes great responsibility.'" Her grin is a bright flash in the dull gray light of the morning. "I think I might know how to help, though."

★ ★ ★

"No way," Gabriel says, and I bristle, straightening my spine to reach my full height. I really wish my full height wasn't so pathetic, though.

"Who says you get a vote?"

"Come on, Olivia, you can't think this is a good idea." Gabriel turns to her, arms folded across his chest. He looks like a stubborn little kid with the crease mark from the couch cushion still striping one cheek and his shirt buttoned wrong.

"It was my idea," she says mildly, "so I'm pretty okay with it, actually."

"Olivia!"

"Enough, Gabriel," I snap. His mouth falls open, but I keep going. "I have to take care of this. You get that, right? And I don't have forever, not after yesterday. So we're going. And we'll see you when we get back and we *haven't* been killed by Danny eating our brains or whatever it is you're scared of."

His jaw is set so tight I'm surprised he can get words out. "I just want to help."

"But you can't! I mean, thank you, but how exactly do you think it's going to help to come with us, so Danny can freak out in the car? Or to leave Danny here with you, so he can freak out in the apartment?"

"I managed yesterday," he protests, and glances

toward his bedroom door.

Danny is still asleep, which is the only thing I can bring myself to call the way he hasn't moved an inch on Gabriel's bed since he lay down. He won't be forever, though. I have no idea how long my spell will last, which is why he's coming with Olivia and me.

"And you looked like you went ten rounds with Holyfield by the time I showed up," I argue, trying not to shout. I'm already vibrating a little bit, nerves and hope and anxiety mixed like a foul soup in my gut. "You didn't even have a moment to call and tell me he woke up."

"Gabriel, sometimes the most helpful thing you can do is step back," Olivia says quietly. She's perched on the stool at the breakfast bar, bag and car keys already on the counter beside her.

"Spare me the touchy-feely yoga wisdom, Liv," Gabriel snaps.

My mouth is the one to fall open this time, but Olivia just shakes her head and sighs. "He's always pouty when he doesn't get his way," she says to me.

His answer to that is to stride out of the room and slam the bathroom door behind him.

"Oh, real mature. My hero."

Olivia stops me before I head into Gabriel's room for Danny. "He means well," she says. "He really cares about you, and it's hard for him that he can't make this easier for you. Cut him a little slack, okay?"

Considering the things she could be saying to me about my own mistakes, it's pretty mild, and I nod at her. I'm sure she doesn't want me to, like, promise her my firstborn child or something, but at this point I'm so grateful for her understanding, I'm ready to at least build a shrine in her honor.

And if the person we're going to see today can help me figure out what to do about Danny, I'm going to be building it pretty soon.

"Are you ready?" she says, and stands up.

"I think so." I take a deep breath. "I mean, I just hope he wakes up in a cooperative mood." I want to say that I wish I could be sure he'll wake up at all, but that's not entirely true, as horrible as it sounds.

So instead I open the door to Gabriel's room and go in to sit on the side of the bed. Danny's cold and still as always, his long lashes brushing his cheeks. One hand lies palm up on the comforter, and I take it in mine, rubbing it gently.

"Danny," I whisper, leaning down to press the word to his lips. "Danny, wake up."

He doesn't stir, and for a moment it's just as terrifying as Ryan's phone call last summer, when I heard the word *dead*. It doesn't matter that Danny and I can't be together the way I wanted to, that everyone's life would be easier if he just kept sleeping. I loved him, still love him, and God, this is going to suck so very much no matter what.

This time, though, I want a chance to say good-bye.

"Danny," I say again, louder now, and concentrate on the energy inside me, drawing it tight and neat. "Wake up now, Danny."

I have to scramble out of the way, because he sits up immediately, eyes opening slowly, as if he hasn't been in something like a coma since almost six o'clock last night.

"Wren," he says, and his smile is just as slow. But a moment later, it dims. "Wren."

I wish there was a way to make him forget again, to take him back to the moments before the accident, when there was nothing but music on the radio and the wind through the open windows and the sweet rush of a few beers in his blood, but the thought of using more magic to rearrange what's in his head also terrifies me.

"Hi." I grip his hand tighter so he keeps looking at me, and I give my best smile. "Let's go for a ride."

Beside me on the backseat of Olivia's car, Danny shuts his eyes and lets his head fall back. "It feels good. The air."

I hold his hand tighter, meeting Olivia's eyes in the rearview mirror. He didn't question me when I explained that she was my friend, and he didn't balk at the car, even though the last car he remembers must be Becker's. As long as I'm holding on to him, he seems pretty calm, but it still feels dangerous to have him out like this. In the unforgiving daylight, he looks even paler than usual. His dark eyes are too flat, expressionless.

She turns her gaze back to the road, and I try not to squirm. We've already been driving for a half hour, and we have at least another thirty miles on the highway.

Rosalie Lanvin is the name of the woman she's taking me to see. "A sort of family friend," Olivia had explained, without really explaining at all. "She has the same kind of power you do, and she's got a hell of a lot more experience with it."

This morning, I jumped at the idea. And it's not that I've changed my mind, not really. But the sensation of the car speeding down the highway, taking me farther and farther away from town, away from home, is a little sobering. I glanced at my silenced phone once after I got up, and found eight voice mail messages and eleven texts. I didn't open any of them.

Skipping school is one thing, but disappearing all night? Part of me is surprised our neighborhood is still standing. My mother doesn't even know Gabriel exists.

It's frightening, feeling like I've been completely

untethered, with no one in the world knowing where I am but Olivia and Gabriel. And what's more, the woman we're going to see could be the one to give me the answers I need to say good-bye to Danny forever. I want that, I do, but if I close my eyes the way Danny has, the sensation of the moving car feels a lot like speeding toward the moment when he'll really be gone, for good this time.

Beside me, he shifts, moving closer, pulling my hand farther into his lap and covering it with his free one. His eyes are still closed, and I don't want to disturb him.

But I take the opportunity to rest my head on his shoulder this time.

CHAPTER TWENTY-ONE

THE HOUSE WHERE OLIVIA PULLS UP IS A SAD little ranch with a weedy front yard and one shutter hanging like a crooked tooth beside the picture window. I wasn't exactly expecting a big Gothic monstrosity with a turret, but the shabby suburban feel of this place is weird, too.

Olivia turns off the car and swivels around to face me. "Okay, she knows we're coming, but I didn't tell her too much. I figured it was better if you did that. And honestly, if she saw it for herself."

"Okay." I sit up, and Danny moves with me, gazing dully at the house through the passenger window.

"She's a little . . . brash." For the first time, Olivia looks unsure, her gray eyes cloudy with concern. "Just be open-minded. I didn't get any of the supernatural bonuses in my family, but I've seen enough to know that Rosalie's pretty good."

She climbs out of the car, and Danny says, "Where are we?" His voice is too loud in the cramped backseat, and there's a vague rumble of unease beneath it.

What am I supposed to say to that? Oh, we're going to see a woman who may be able to help me get rid of you for good? Someone who has powers like mine but hopefully doesn't use them to do shitty, stupid things?

"She's a friend of Olivia's, Danny. It's okay." I have to work to turn on my smile again, making it persuasive and completely confident, as if an hour's drive to a complete stranger's house is something we do every day.

Olivia is waiting on the front steps, and she motions for us to join her. Danny frowns, but when I get out of the car he follows me, his hand still tight around mine. I brush a smear of dirt off the back of his jeans, as if that's going to make everything all right, make him look normal. His skin practically glows phosphorescent, it's so pale.

The door opens mere seconds after Olivia knocks, and the woman on the other side is another surprise.

She's around my mom's age, or maybe a little older, but she's much thicker set, and she's dressed sort of like a PE teacher, in old chinos and a sweatshirt with UMASS emblazoned on the front.

In short, she looks about as much like a witch as I do. It's oddly reassuring.

"Liv," she says, nodding at Olivia before adding, "Your father's not with you, is he?"

Olivia's cheeks bloom pink, but she shakes her head and steps aside to give Rosalie a better view of me. "God, no. This is Wren, and that's Danny."

This is met with a brief grunt as Rosalie's faded brown eyes scan over me. "How old are you, kid?"

"Seventeen." I have no idea if this is good or bad—I feel as if I'm undergoing some sort of test as she searches my face, and suddenly I'm not sure she's even going to invite us in. My throat is dry, and Danny's fingers are so tight around my hand, I'm beginning to lose the feeling in my fingertips.

Rosalie sighs and steps back. "Come on, then. No need to do this in front of the neighbors."

An ancient, overweight beagle lifts his head drowsily when we walk in, and for a moment I'm sure he's simply going to go back to sleep. Instead, he flinches when Danny follows me in, and gets to his feet as quickly as his stubby little legs will allow. His coat is bristling and he's growling low in his throat, showing his stained yellow teeth.

"Interesting," Rosalie says mildly, and tilts her head to watch as the dog's body begins to shake. "Okay, Barker, no worries. Be right back, all." She scoops the dog up, whispering something soothing in his ear, and disappears down the hall, where a door is shut firmly a moment later.

For his part, Danny either hasn't noticed or doesn't care that the dog was ready to rip his throat out, but Olivia is clearly a little freaked. She moves a pile of newspapers off a chair in the corner of the cluttered living room and sits down, studying the car keys she still has clutched in one hand. When Rosalie reappears, Danny and I are still standing awkwardly in the middle of the room like characters who have wandered into the wrong scene in a play.

"Come on in the kitchen, kid," Rosalie calls. "You have a seat," she tells Danny. Like that's going to work. He bristles like a threatened cat, holding on to me tighter still.

"Wren." It sounds like the dog's growl, and I try not to shudder.

"Danny, it's okay." I tug on his hand until he looks away from Rosalie, who, to her credit, seems remarkably unimpressed. *"Danny."*

When I finally have his attention, I focus and push my power through our joined hands, thinking *Stay* at him as hard as I can. It tingles beneath my skin, briefly hot but promising a burn, and Danny stares until he lets go of my hand and backs up, landing on the sofa. He blinks, but he doesn't say another word.

"Just like magic," Rosalie says when I glance back at her, and the corner of her mouth folds into an ugly smirk.

Not fair. I choke back the angry energy that flares to life and follow her into the kitchen. It smells like dog food and burnt coffee, but it at least looks clean. I take the chair opposite hers at the table.

"So." She opens a bottle of diet soda with a short hiss and drinks a mouthful. "You wanna tell me about your undead Romeo in there?"

If this is part of the test, I'm definitely going to fail. For a minute I just gape, with no idea how to answer, since the only things I want to say would be ruder than even I can get away with.

"Hey, if you can't do the time," she says, watching my face. "Olivia didn't give me the whole story, but it's pretty clear that at least one thing that boy is missing is a heartbeat. And I'm not sure what it is you want me to do about it."

"Help me," I blurt out without thinking. "Help me figure out how to . . ."

The words trail off into the silence. There's never going to be a good way to end that sentence.

"How to what?" Rosalie barks, and leans closer, eyes narrowed. "Kid, if you had the juice to bring that six-foot cutie back from the dead, you're a couple pay grades above me."

I know it's not possible, but it suddenly feels like all the air has been sucked out of the room. My lungs burn with the effort of breathing, shuddering as my heart bangs between them. She was supposed to help me, and if she can't, if she won't . . .

"A spell." It's a rough croak, but it's all I can manage for a minute. Rosalie just sits there, impassive, as I struggle to get air into my lungs and stop panicking. "I thought you could give me a spell."

She snorts, an ugly noise. "Are you kidding? What do you think there is, some *Big Book of Incantations* out there with all the spells you'll ever need?"

Before I can say anything, Rosalie plunges ahead, her meaty hands joining in now. "One," she says, holding up her index finger. "Most practitioners are wannabes who have about as much power inside them as a wind-up toy. Two, most people who do have power don't even know it. Three, the rest of us do our homework, and hone our craft with a lot of boring, infuriating trial and error."

Those three thick fingers waggle at me briefly before her hand closes into a loose fist and drops to the table. I swallow, focusing on the scarred Formica instead of Rosalie's face. You don't have to be psychic to know she's not done yet.

"I don't know how you pulled this off, kid, but there is no easy answer to an undead boyfriend." She shrugs and adds, "Not unless you have an ax handy and you know how to use it."

A low, hurt sound vibrates in my throat, and Rosalie shrugs again.

I can't help glancing out toward the living room, picturing Danny on the sofa, his long limbs sprawled loosely, his face blank and cold. She may not be able to, but I can still see the Danny I knew, the one I loved, warm with summer sweat, laughing as he leans in to kiss me with grape soda on his lips. "You're crazy," I whisper.

"I'm practical," she counters. "But I'm not really serious. For one, you'd probably fall over backward just trying to lift an ax."

I'm seething, trying not to cry. I don't care what anyone says—this is not some zombie flick, and I'm not getting rid of Danny like he's some vicious, brain-hungry freak. "You're so not funny."

"I'm not trying to be, kid." She leans back and folds her arms over her chest. "Look, tell me how you did this."

Her voice has finally lost most of its nasty edge, and a thrill of hope raises the hair on the back of my neck. I stumble and backtrack and skip around and nearly lose it at least twice, but I manage to tell her everything—about my mother's power, my own, the things I've taught myself to do, the car accident, and finally the spell in the graveyard. By the time I'm done, I'm hoarse and exhausted, and she gets up without a word and brings me a glass of water.

I gulp it down gratefully. "So?"

She raises her eyebrows. "Like I said, you and apparently your whole family make me look like a rookie who's not even going to make it through the minors."

"Great, thanks." I can't help it now. A few scalding tears roll down one cheek and I swipe them away, hating that I'm crying in front of her. "I get it, okay? I'm going to the Hall of Fame for worst home run ever, right?"

Before she can answer, something crashes in the living room, and Olivia's voice carries into the kitchen. "Um, Wren?"

I stumble out of my chair and into the other room. Danny has kicked over the coffee table, and magazines and books and a dying potted plant have spilled over the green shag carpet. He's struggling, trying to get up, but my impromptu spell won't let him.

If the look he gives me is any indication, he knows it, too, and he's pissed.

"Danny, stop."

"You're the one . . ." He wriggles, kicking his feet out again. His hands are clenched into fists as he tries to push against the magic holding him to the sofa.

"Just relax," I'm begging as fresh tears spill down my face. He's as furious as he was in the park, charging at me like a bull, and if he managed to kick over the coffee table, I'm not sure how long the loose bond will last. "Please, Danny. We can go in a minute, but you have to calm down, *please*."

"Let me *go*."

Three simple words, and yet they stand for everything I haven't been able to do since he died. Grief and regret flood through me, and it's like trying to walk away from the wind—I can't escape it, so I let it slam into me instead.

"Stop," I scream, just like the morning in the park, and Danny collapses as if his strings have been cut. He slumps back against the sofa, boneless where he was rigid and straining just a moment ago, eyes still open, staring at the ceiling without seeing it.

The silence rings, stretching out so long, I flinch when Olivia makes a soft, wordless noise.

"Oh, kid." Behind me, Rosalie puts a hand on my shoulder. I can't let myself lean into the weight of it, because if I do, I'm pretty sure I'll break into a million tiny, heartbroken pieces.

Olivia is trembling. "It's okay," I say. My chest is still heaving. "He's just sort of . . . sleeping. Like before, when Gabriel and I brought him back to your place. But you have to help me get him into the car, okay? Olivia?"

She nods.

"You go get the car open," Rosalie says to her. "I'll help with this one."

Since Olivia isn't much bigger than I am, I don't argue, but it's still ridiculous and completely undignified, the two of us struggling under Danny's weight as we push and pull and drag him out to the driveway and into the car.

Dead weight, the voice in my head supplies, accusing, and I bite my lip hard enough to draw fresh tears so it will go away.

By the time Danny is flopped in the backseat, unseeing and motionless, we're both panting, but Rosalie stops me before I climb into the front passenger seat. Olivia's already inside, staring straight ahead, hands gripping the wheel.

"Full moon is Monday night," Rosalie says. Her ruddy cheeks are redder now, and sweat is gleaming on her forehead even in the chilly afternoon air. "I wouldn't wait, kid."

As if. Even I'm not balking anymore. "But how . . . ?"

"Whatever you did, twist it." She shrugs, and the wind tosses her hair back. "Do it backward. Think about the spell you created and what you want this spell to do. Think about . . . giving him some peace. Just . . . choose your words wisely."

The fingertips of my clenched right hand push into the scar on my palm, and I nod. "Thank you."

"Hey, it's nothing, really." When she shrugs this time, it's a little helpless-looking. "And good luck."

There's no doubt I'm going to need it.

CHAPTER TWENTY-TWO

"I'M SORRY ROSALIE COULDN'T HELP."

Olivia's tone is wistful by the time we're back at the apartment, which surprises me. She didn't have to help me. She could have run screaming the other way, and instead she's sorry. She's as delicately made as Gabriel, and she looks a lot like a light breeze would knock her over, but there's steel in her bones.

Just like her brother.

"I know there was probably a sweet boy in there once," she says, shrugging sadly, "but he's angry, Wren. He's angry and confused, and he's *dead*. And what's worse, now he seems to know it."

I don't know what I'm supposed to say except "I'm sorry," and I'm pretty sure that's getting old for everyone involved.

"What exactly did Rosalie say?" Gabriel asks.

"That there's a full moon Monday night." Olivia shrugs and glances at the closed door to Gabriel's bedroom. "Do you think you can be ready by then?"

"I don't have a choice."

"I wish I could do something more to help," she tells me before taking a sighing breath and relaxing. "But for now I'm going to treat myself to a very stiff drink. Or four. And say a prayer of thanks that I wasn't the one who got the woo-woo powers in my family."

When she disappears into the kitchen, Gabriel comes to sit beside me on the sofa. "You want to tell me exactly what happened?"

"Not really." I shrug when he glares at me. "I'm tired of talking. I'm tired of thinking, and crying, and worrying, and breathing, if you want the truth. But I meant what I said. On Monday this is all going to be over."

"Are you sure?" He sits forward, elbows on his knees, his brow furrowed, and I wish he wasn't so stupidly beautiful that even in concern he's gorgeous to look at.

It doesn't mean his worrying doesn't get annoying, though. "Gabriel."

"I'm serious," he protests, gray eyes wide and honest. "What if the spell doesn't work? What if you can't come up with a spell at all? What if he—"

"*Gabriel.*" Danny never made me as furious as Gabriel sometimes can. "Give me some credit, okay? I mean, I know it was awful and I shouldn't have done it, but I did figure out how to bring him back in the first place. Just stop, okay? I *will* take care of this."

"I know that. But this is different."

"How?"

"This time you have to get Danny to the graveyard, and he isn't exactly Mr. Cooperative when he's awake, if you haven't noticed. What do you think he's going to do when you start chanting some spell? Just sit back and wait to die? Again?"

Damn it. I haven't thought that far ahead, but then I haven't really thought much further than the next ten minutes for days. I glance up as Olivia leaves the kitchen and goes into her room, shutting the door firmly behind her.

"Look, I'll figure it out," I snap, pushing up off the sofa. "It's not your problem anyway."

"Wren, I just want to—"

"Help. I know, I've heard." He flinches, and it's meaner than I meant to be, but I don't want to make him any more a part of this than he already is. There are some things you don't want anyone to see. And I'm beginning to feel like my whole life is one of them.

"Why do you care so much?" I ask, even though I can't face him and I'm talking to my feet, the scuffed toes of my Docs against the dull wood floor. "I mean, honestly. Why do you even like me?"

"Wren." It's my turn to flinch when he steps up beside me and lays his hand on the small of my back. I want it so much, to count on it there, to lean back into it, to let him take some of my weight. But I can't, not now, not with Danny in one room and Olivia in the other.

Not when I don't even understand what it is he sees in me. The only things I see anymore when I look in the mirror make me want to run away.

"Do you want, like, an itemized list or the *Reader's Digest* version?" he says, leaning close enough that I can feel his breath tickle my cheek.

I open my mouth to answer him just as the phone in the kitchen rings, a shrill surprise. He drops his hand as if we've been doing a lot more than just standing close together, and when it keeps ringing, he bolts toward the kitchen to pick it up.

I wrap my arms around myself and wait, even though I don't know what for. Whatever Gabriel feels for me, I can't let it matter to me. I have to go home eventually, for one thing, and face my mother. I have to apologize to Jess and Darcia, if they'll let me. And I have to create a spell that will send Danny back to death.

It doesn't matter that the only thing I want right now is to put my arms around Gabriel, to feel his arms around me and his mouth on mine, to let him take some of my fear and grief and swallow it for me.

Real love is supposed to be more than solace, more than a way to forget. I had real love once, I think, and what did I do with it? I made Danny do those things for me when he was the one who needed peace the most.

When Gabriel touches my arm, I'm so lost in my thoughts, I jump. He holds out the phone, a cheap portable handset, and frowns. "It's for you."

My mother, I think, my heart sinking into my stomach with a nauseating thud, but I take it anyway. It's not like I can hide forever.

"Hello?"

"Wren, don't hang up."

As if. It's Aunt Mari, and I'm so stunned with relief, I stumble forward a step. "How did you . . . ? I mean, how could you know . . . ?"

"You're not the only one with magic in this family." I can hear the smile in her voice, but she's tired, too, I can tell. "I have a proposal for you."

★ ★ ★

Bliss is quiet when I walk in, only two kids from school at a table in the front window, and Mari at another along the wall, two tall mugs of coffee already set out. Trevor's behind the counter as always, and he looks up when the bell jingles.

"You're not working tonight."

"You're lucky I come in on my day off. This place is really hopping." It feels good to snap at him the way I always do, especially when he just rolls his eyes, the way he always does.

"Nothing's on the house," he calls as I walk over to Mari's table and pull out a chair. He's lying, of course, but the tough-guy act is one of his favorite things.

"I see Trevor hasn't lost his charm," Mari says drily, loud enough for him to hear.

"You either," he retorts, and a moment later he's tapping on his keyboard as if a little banter was just what he needed to get his creative juices flowing.

I hang my bag over the back of my chair and look at Mari properly for the first time in months. I haven't seen her since a few weeks after Danny's funeral, and at the time I was spending every free minute furtively studying spell books. She was the last person I wanted to see then.

She looks good, though strain shows in the dark blue smears under her eyes and the tangled knot of curls on top of her head. There are only two explanations for her knowing that I took off, and my bet is actually on Mom calling her rather than Robin. It's hardly the most important thing right now, but it's a small sign of hope.

"You okay?" She reaches across the table to put her hand on mine, and all I can do is nod. My throat is suddenly choked with tears again.

"More or less, huh?" she says. Her smile is fond. "Your mom's on the 'less' end of the spectrum at the moment, and so is Robin. She said she texted you and you didn't answer."

Oh God. Robin must be completely freaked out. "I haven't even looked at my phone since yesterday."

"I figured. And you might be mad, but I told them you agreed to meet me here. Just so they'd know you were okay."

"I was going to go home, really," I say, but it's a hoarse whisper. Sometime later, I'm going to look into having my tear ducts removed. I haven't cried this often ever, and I hate how weak and helpless it makes me feel. Having power explode out of me is bad enough, I don't need to be leaking tears every minute.

"I'd like to take you home when we're done here," Mari says. It sounds like a suggestion, but I know it isn't.

"What did Mom tell you?" I pick up my mug and

blow across the top, just so I won't have to look at Mari's face.

"I'm more interested in what you want to tell me, to be honest."

That's a great big nothing, but there's no way I'm going to get away with that. I gulp at my coffee, which is still a little too hot, and splutter a little. "It's nothing," I finally manage. "I mean, okay, it's not nothing, but I'm handling it. And like I told Mom, I'm not on drugs, and I'm not pregnant, and I'm not wanted by the police, so . . ."

"Good to know." There's that dry tone again, paired this time with a raised eyebrow. "Come on, Wren, this is me. What's going on?"

I hate that I can't tell her anything. But I can't bear the look I know I'll see on her face if I admit what I've done. As far as Mom's turned from her own power, Mari equally celebrates hers. But she's never used it lightly, and there's no way she would understand that I used mine to bring someone back from the dead, even Danny.

"I went a little crazy," I venture, glancing toward the counter in case Trevor is listening in, which he loves to do when he's frustrated and can't come up with the right sentence. "After Danny, I mean. And . . . I met a new guy. So that's been a little . . . strange."

It's nowhere near the whole truth, but it's part of it. Admitting that Gabriel figures into the last couple of days is even harder than I expected. It still feels like a betrayal.

Naturally, Trevor caught that juicy tidbit, and he looks as pleased as Mari looks wistful.

"Oh, sweetie." She reaches for my hand again and squeezes my fingers gently. "That has to be hard. But no matter how much you loved Danny, life doesn't stop at seventeen. And you deserve another chance at finding someone. More than one, I bet."

I knew that admitting I liked another boy would seem to explain everything, and part of me hates to use Gabriel that way. But I can't tell Mari the whole truth. It's selfish, I know, but if I'm going to fix it, I don't want them ever to know how bad I messed up.

They all know that I am the girl who touches the hot stove and drops the eggs. They don't need to know that I'm also the girl who thought love came with ownership papers, who decided to try to cheat death so her own life wouldn't feel so empty, no matter what it would do to the boy she loved.

Mari's waiting for me to agree, I can tell, so I nod. I'm beginning to feel numb, but the day's not even close to over. I sip my coffee slowly. The longer it takes to drink, the longer it will be before Mari drives me home, and that's some comfort, anyway. She's been understanding, but I doubt Mom is going to be.

"Trevor, you got any of Geoff's iced maple cookies left over there?" Mari calls.

"Could be," he says, and shrugs. He likes to give her a hard time, because he likes to give everyone a hard time, but I think she also fascinates him. She's been coming into the café longer than I have—she's actually the one who introduced me to it. She's been a preschool teacher for years, but she's always doing something else on the side—making jewelry one day, singing in a band another, once even appearing in an indie horror movie shot in the city. I think he's jealous of how fully she lives her life, and I don't really blame him.

"Wrap up a dozen, if you can find them, that is." She winks at me when he groans and gets off his stool. "I think we might need some sugary goodness later."

If you ask me, it's a little like frosting a cake made out of sewage and old socks, but I'm not arguing. When I face Mom, I'm going to be grateful for any help I can get.

CHAPTER TWENTY-THREE

ROBIN MUST HEAR THE CAR PULL INTO THE driveway, because she bursts out the front door and is running down the porch steps before I can even get out.

I stagger backward when she attack-hugs, her sturdy arms wrapped so tightly around me, I can hardly breathe.

"Don't ever, ever do that again." Her voice shakes, but the rest of her is fiercely sturdy, clinging to me like a monkey. "Promise me."

"I do." I kiss the top of her head, and her hair is earthy and unwashed. "I'm so sorry, Binny. So sorry."

She squeezes me, hard, and my ribs pinch in protest. "You better be. Where *were* you?"

"Not far, really. I'm okay." I take a shaky breath when she finally lets go, and Mari walks around the car to grab Robin's hand.

"Inside, huh?" She tugs and Robin follows, but not before grabbing my hand so we're walking up the porch steps like a crooked daisy chain.

And at the top, standing just inside the screen door, is Mom.

"We brought cookies," Mari says brightly, but Mom doesn't even seem to hear her. She's staring at me, only at me, and steps aside just far enough to let Mari and Robin into the house before she says a word.

"Wren."

I can hear so much in the single word, love and regret and relief and even anger, and I wonder if it will sound the same if I say, "Mom." Instead, I push the screen aside and walk in. We're only inches apart, so close I can smell the clean cotton of her shirt, the faint citrus of her shampoo, but the distance seems like miles. Just as I decide I should keep walking, she grabs me and pulls me against her.

"I guess we need to talk," she murmurs into my hair, and I nod.

"You're not off the hook here, you know," she adds as she sets me away from her. "I'm still angry."

"I know." I steady my voice. "So am I."

Her mouth twists as if she's trying not to smile. "Fair enough."

The fire is hypnotic, long fingers of flame reaching for the flue, the grate, flicking and snapping with the wind outside. Now that Mari's taken Robin upstairs and Mom and I are settled on the hearth, it's hard to know where to begin. I watch the fire instead, holding my palms up to let the heat seep in.

"So this is awkward," Mom says mildly, and I can't help but snort. "I guess I should have read one of those parenting books, you know?" She's looking at the flames, too, instead of at me, and I can't tell if she's joking or not. "*Teenage Rebellion and You* or something like that."

"I'm not rebelling, Mom."

"Aren't you? I made something forbidden and you decided to go ahead and do it anyway. Unless this isn't about the magic." She finally turns to face me, and maybe the fire is magic, too. As the flickering shadows move over her face, I can see myself there in the set of her jaw, and Robin in the hair falling across her forehead, and Mari and even Gram in the shape of her eyes.

"It is," I admit, wrapping my arms around my knees. "And it isn't."

"I'm too tired for riddles, kiddo." She gives me a wan

smile, and tucks a stray feather of hair behind my ear. "It's been a long couple of days."

"I know, and I really am sorry. I didn't mean to make you worry. I didn't mean . . ." I shake my head and rest my chin on my knees. "I didn't mean for a lot of things to happen."

"Can you tell me what they are?"

"I'd rather not?"

She sighs. "But you're not pregnant, and you're not on drugs, and you're not wanted by the police."

"Right."

"You know, if you want to be honest from here on out, about our power and everything else, it's a two-way street."

I nod. "Can't we just start fresh, from right now? I promise you, I'm okay. Or I will be. I'm trying to clean up my own mistakes here, and that has to count for something, right?"

She sets her jaw, and the flames in the hearth jump a little higher. "It's not going to be that easy, Wren. I'm not just letting you off the hook free and clear because you had a bad day."

"I'm not asking you to!"

She levels a gaze at me, and for a second our power and our anger is tangible, crackling in the air between us. "Oh no? But you won't tell me what went on this weekend? You have to understand that it's hard for me not to know what you're going through."

"It's hard for me not to know, well, a lot of things," I say carefully, and glance sideways to watch her face. She doesn't smile but she doesn't flinch, either, and that's good, I guess. "Things about what I can do, what I am, what . . . the limits are, I guess."

She swivels around to face me then, and we're like one person, reflected in a mirror—her arms around her bent knees, her chin propped on top of them.

"You know who you are, I hope." She tilts her head, thoughtful, as if she's testing the shape and weight of the words to come. "You're a bright, imaginative girl with a lot of special talents."

She's so not getting off that easy. I arch a brow at her. "Come on, Mom. Special talents are playing the violin really well and scoring goals every game. What we are is different."

"You're right. And different doesn't mean bad, all evidence around this house the last few years to the contrary."

I peel chipped dark purple polish off my thumbnail. "You know I remember, right? When Robin was born, before Dad left, when Mari and Gram were here all the time? It was a part of us then. It wasn't weird or wrong. I thought it was strange that other moms couldn't make flowers grow or put fairy lights up on the ceiling."

She's silent for a long time, remembering, I think, and the sadness on her face hurts. But I'm not going to let that stop me. If she wants honesty, then she can go first.

"Is it why Dad left? Or is that why you stopped, I don't know, being so open about what we are?"

She sighs and narrows her eyes at me. "This is not the conversation we need to have right now. You screwed up, and I'm not taking the responsibility for it, and I'm not letting you change the subject."

I scrub my hands over my face, trying to push down the need to shout, to throw something. "But that's what you always say! So when can we talk about it? This is *my* life, Mom."

She bites her bottom lip before she speaks again, and I can see the angry white teeth marks in it pinking up. "Your dad had really good reasons for leaving."

I don't know what I was expecting her to say, but it wasn't that. Good reasons? What does that even mean?

"Good? Good enough to leave and never call again? To act like Robin and I don't even exist?"

Mom tilts her head back, as if the answer is written on the ceiling. "It's complicated, Wren."

I bet it is, but I still want to *know*. It's a huge piece of my life that's been covered up with a sheet, sitting in the middle of the room all these years while we were expected to ignore it.

"Was it you?" What I really want to say is, *Tell me it wasn't me*. But I can't make my mouth form those words.

Mom doesn't try to mask the hurt in her voice. "No, it wasn't me. It wasn't you girls, either. And if you think I haven't missed him every day since he left, if you think I don't still love him, you're wrong."

For a second, all I can see is Danny's face, dozens of them, superimposed on each other: Danny laughing, Danny with his bottom lip between his teeth as he draws, Danny leaning forward to kiss me, Danny pale and cold and still. I get it, or I think I do, but it doesn't help.

I can see my dad's face, too, as he leaned close to read to me before bed. When I close my eyes, I can feel the bony set of his shoulders when he lifted me up for a ride, and breathe in the dark, smoky scent of his shirts.

Whoever decided that love should hurt sucks.

It's been silent for too long, and I watch as Mom wipes a tear off her cheek. Whoever decided that life should hurt sucks even more.

"I'm sorry," I say. I hate that she's been carrying this around for so long, but so have I. "I don't get it. How can there be a good reason never to talk to your kids again? How can you still love him after that?"

It's a stupid question. I still love him, or what I remember of him. It's the foundation of what I feel for him, even if I've painted over it with rage and betrayal and confusion.

"You're going to have to ask him to explain it, I think," Mom says carefully, and turns her head to face me again. Nothing is hidden—for the first time in a long time, everything she's feeling is right there in her eyes. "And I can help you, when you're ready."

For a moment, my ears ring with pounding blood just like they did when Ryan told me Danny was dead. It's too unbelievable, too strange, words that make sense on their own but not strung into that sentence.

"Help me?" My voice breaks a little, and I sit up straight, blinking at her. "You know where he is?"

She doesn't even try to soften the blow. "I do. Well, I know how to get in touch with him, to be more precise."

"All this time?" I struggle to my feet, walking off the tingling thrills of energy coursing through me. "All these years, and you never said anything? What the hell, Mom?"

"Wren."

"No, Mom!" I won't cry, I *won't*. I'm too angry

anyway, an icy blue in my veins, crackling and brittle. "All these years I thought he hated us! I thought we weren't good enough! And you've been talking to him?"

"Come here." I didn't even hear her get up, but Mom is suddenly beside me, taking my hands in hers and turning me to face the fire. "Do it, let it go. It's not good to let it build up, believe me."

I'm not sure what she means at first, but then she uncurls my clenched fingers and spreads my hands out. I'm not even thinking when I close my eyes and just let it come, the way she said, and a moment later the fire hisses furiously as icicles plunge into the flames.

It's exactly the opposite of what happened that day in the basement after Danny's funeral, and I can see that she knows it. For a minute I can't speak—the relief is so sweet, all that rage fired off into the heart of the fire. When Mom puts her arm around my shoulder, I don't protest. The mad is still there, but it's only simmering now, distant, in another room where I can't really feel its heat.

"It's not exactly like what you're imagining," she says, and leads me to the sofa, where she sits beside me and pulls my head onto her shoulder. "I've kept him updated about you and your sister, because he wants to know. He loves you both, but he felt that it was better for you to be without him. He did what he did out of love, Wren. Regardless of fairy tales, love doesn't always mean a happy ending."

I bury my face against her, but it's not my dad I'm thinking of. I'm picturing Danny as I left him on Gabriel's bed, frozen in place, still slightly dirty from his midnight wandering, his lips blue and thin, so different from the warm, lush mouth that I used to kiss.

If I love him, the right thing to do is to let him go. And hope that wherever he goes, he doesn't remember that I didn't love him enough to leave him in peace in the first place.

There might not be a happy ending for me, but I'm going to give one to Danny. I just hope it's not too late.

CHAPTER TWENTY-FOUR

SUNDAY MORNING FEELS LIKE A STRANGE dream. Mari slept over, so there are four of us at the breakfast table, and watching Mari and Mom laugh together as they make waffles is a little surreal after all the times I wished for the exact same thing. Robin is sort of baffled, since she doesn't remember them this way at all, elbowing each other and goofing around, acting like sisters instead of stiff, uncomfortable strangers, but I can tell she's happy about it, too.

It's not perfect, of course. But when I went to bed last night, I stopped in the hall outside Mom's room, and I could still hear them talking.

"It's not something you can ignore," Mari had said, so softly I could barely hear it, not that I should have been pressed up against the wall beside the door eavesdropping in the first place. "Sam knows that, too."

Sam. My dad.

Mom's answer was nothing more than a vague murmur, too low for me to understand, and I wondered if they were talking about our power.

Whatever it was, I went to sleep that night thinking that Mom hadn't really let go of the man she loved, either. Maybe we weren't so different, after all. I wanted to let that comfort me, but Monday night loomed over everything else, a dark, distinct point on the horizon.

It's hard to shake the shadow of it, even sitting at the kitchen table with a plate of fresh waffles drowning in butter and syrup in front of me. But I make the effort, hanging around to make up for my disappearing act, and Robin's gratitude bubbles over in funny ways, sweetening the orange juice in my glass and gleaming on the basket of tiny baby pumpkins Mom brought, shinier and deeper in color all of a sudden.

For once, Mom says, "Pretty," when she spots them, and runs a finger over the fat one on top of the basket. Robin blushes, and at the counter, Aunt Mari smiles over her coffee mug.

I want to hold on to all of it, but I have to check on Danny, and Mom doesn't stop me, even though I don't say where I'm going. I'm a little surprised, but she just follows me to the front door and lays her cheek against mine. Robin and Aunt Mari are settled on the sofa watching a movie while Mari brushes Robin's hair.

"Home by dinner," Mom says. "And school tomorrow, no question. We'll deal with consequences later."

It's more than I could have asked for, even if cutting school isn't really a big deal in my head. Not compared with everything else I've done.

It hurts that I'll never be able to tell her what happened. At least not anytime soon.

It's hard enough for me, when I get to Gabriel's, to see Danny still lying on Gabriel's bed, in the same position. Nothing can be that still for so long. Nothing living, anyway.

I lie beside him on the bed, fitting myself up against the cool, motionless length of him. My hand rests over his heart, but I don't expect to feel the thump of it there anymore.

And then I start talking. It's natural—talking is what we used to do, endlessly, on the phone, walking home from school or the café, curled up together on the sofa. I don't think he can hear me, but it doesn't matter. There are things I want to say, and I don't want to hide anything from him anymore.

"Becker misses you," I tell him. The words are muffled because my mouth is pressed against his chest. "He feels so guilty, Danny. And he's so messed up now. I go to see him sometimes, and so does Ryan. He misses you, too. We went to see Becker together once, but it was too weird. There was this big empty place where you were supposed to be instead."

I only pause to brush at the tears on my cheek. They're making a wet spot on Danny's T-shirt. "I thought I was doing the right thing, you know? Well, maybe not. But I wanted it so much. I just wanted *you*. I missed you. I still miss you, so much. It's not fair."

I can't say anything after that, because I'm crying too hard, but after a little while I layer another spell on top of the one that's keeping him there on the bed, still and silent. A minute later, Gabriel pushes the door open a few inches, and I look up with my cheeks still wet.

"Everything okay?"

I just stare at him until he backs away. I mean, I know it's a lot to ask, having the girl you like cuddling her undead boyfriend in your room, but if Danny had woken up raging and dangerous, I'm pretty sure Gabriel would have heard the commotion.

I know I should have a little more sympathy for him, and when I finally get up and go into the living room, I remind myself how generous he's been. He looks awful, with his tired eyes focused so carefully on me, and for a minute I want to curl up with him. Let him lay me down on the sofa and hold me, let everything pour out into the worn fabric of his Rutgers T-shirt and let him smooth me out with his hands.

But there's not a lot left. I'm so hollow inside that I barely do more than nod when I leave, and all night, sitting up with the spell books and working on what I have to do, I have to push both faces out of my mind, Danny's and Gabriel's.

I'm up so late that I'm almost late for school on Monday, and Gabriel sits on the bench next to me in the principal's office during homeroom. I'm trying as hard as I can to close myself off, because I can't be sure he won't peek inside to see what I'm feeling, no matter what he says about respecting boundaries.

"Detention, you think? Or a day's suspension?" His voice is low and a little rough.

I don't even look at him, although I can't help seeing the sharp angle of his jaw out of the corner of my eye. "No clue."

Judging by his frustrated huff, he's not happy with

that answer. And I'm ashamed of myself, because I don't want to hurt him, but I can't keep arguing the same things over and over.

Except he won't let them go.

Case in point: "I know you don't want to talk about this, but—"

"So stop bringing it up," I hiss, glancing up from under my lashes when the secretary looks at us sternly.

"You don't understand how dangerous this could be," Gabriel says, even lower now, leaning sideways and crowding into my space.

"And you don't understand that it's not your problem." I shift as far away from him as I can, and he stiffens.

"What happened, Wren? What did I do?"

The door to the principal's office opens, and the secretary says, "You can go in now."

Which means I don't have to say, *You made me want you, and I don't trust myself not to screw that up, too,* which is the only truth that matters.

We get off with a warning, which I'm grateful for since I need to be home after school finishing the spell. I expect the day to drag, but I'm so preoccupied with catching up in my classes that it's lunchtime before I know it. The instinct to go hide in the library is pretty strong, but I can't do that. If I'm going to make things right with Jess and Darcia, I have to actually talk to them.

I'm not expecting Jess to be waiting outside the cafeteria doors, though. I choke back a flicker of startled power that threatens to explode out of me, and only clutch my books tighter to my chest as I walk up to her.

"I tried calling. And texting."

She flips her hair over her shoulder, all casual and cool, but she's not actually looking me in the eye. "Yeah, well. So did I. On Friday."

I hate this. I've known Jess since I was eight, and I don't want to lose her. I don't think I realized until recently how close I've come.

"I can only say I'm sorry, Jess." I take a step closer. "And I am. I can't . . . I can't really explain what happened, but the thing is, I can't really be sorry about that part. I want us to be friends, I always want us to be friends, but we're not kids anymore. Some stuff is going to be private. And . . . I guess I want you to respect that, even if I don't deserve it."

I'm nearly breathless, because it all comes out in a rush, but at least I said it. Someone jostles me as they push by in the crowd entering the cafeteria, but I don't move. I'm watching Jess, and I'm not going anywhere until she says something.

As long as she doesn't simply walk away.

Her expression shifts, as fluid as running water, but she finally meets my gaze. "How are secrets okay if we're friends?"

My chin goes up, just an inch. I hate being shorter than anyone but fourth graders. "Are you really standing there telling me I know everything about you? Seriously?"

She bites her lip then, but she doesn't lie. It's a start.

"Look, Danny dying . . . it fucked me up, okay? I get that. But I'm trying. And I just want there to be room to keep some things private, and not be, well, judged." My heart is still pounding, but I've gotten this far and I'm not turning back. "I love you, Jess, but we're not always going to want the same things. Or feel the same things. We're just not."

"I don't judge you!"

I tilt my head. "Jess."

"Oh, like you don't do the same thing." She's angry again, but she's still not leaving, and part of me wants to grab her arm and hang on until I know she understands.

"When you make out with Eli Harbeck ten minutes after dissing band geeks, what do you think I'm going to do? I'm pretty sure he, like, takes his clarinet to bed at night."

She colors hotly, but I think she's trying not to smile,

because her mouth is twitching like a rabbit's nose. Finally she straightens up and says, "So you're really not going to tell me what happened on Friday?"

I shrug. "Yeah, no."

"But you're okay?" She doesn't wait for me to answer, and adds, "And you weren't, like, just making up that you wanted us to spend the night? I mean, if you're not into hanging out, you should really just say so, because you never used to be mean, Wren, and Dar was really—"

"Jess." I touch her shoulder, because somewhere in there her eyes started darting down the hallway, through the big windows that overlook the courtyard, at a point past my right shoulder. "No. I totally wanted it. And I still do. This Friday, okay? For real. I can guarantee that nothing will happen this time, I promise."

She considers this silently, chewing on her lip the way she used to chew on her fingernails before her mother starting putting some nasty no-biting stuff on them.

"I'm still so mad, you know?" She shakes her head. "I mean, I won't be forever, but I don't think I'm ready to stop yet?"

I can't help laughing a little at that. It's so Jess. And me, too, if I'm honest. "I get it. I'll wait."

★ ★ ★

Darcia nearly cries in World Lit after we talk, which is a little alarming, but she hugs me, too, a crushing bear hug that doesn't seem possible from a girl as reedy as she is. By the time school is over, I'm exhausted.

I'm twirling the dial on my locker when someone taps my shoulder, and I turn around to find Gabriel standing there, tall and stiff and beautiful. His face is as stony as Danny's, and I resist the urge to close my eyes so I don't have to see it.

"I want you to listen to me," he says, and he's not even trying to keep this between us. Across the hall, two sophomores turn around, curious, and I fume.

"And I want you to back off."

"No." It doesn't seem possible, but he straightens up another inch, as if sheer size is going to convince me. "You're being reckless. You don't know what you're doing, and you could get really hurt. Not boo-hoo, broken-heart hurt, either, but *hurt*. You need to let me take care of this for you."

I don't care how big he's trying to seem—fury makes me feel seven feet tall. "Are you kidding? Who are you, my knight in faded denim? I am not some lame princess in a tower who needs to be rescued, thank you very much." I don't even need to put on the scorn; it's completely honest.

He's immovable. "You weren't exactly refusing my help the other night."

If he can't feel the power gathering strength like a storm cloud in me right now, he's a sucktastic psychic. "So? I asked for help because I thought you were a friend. And now I'm telling you to back the fuck off. Because I *don't* need your help with this, no matter what you think."

His cheeks are hot with frustration now, and his eyes are darker, as stormy as the roiling power in my gut. "You are barely five feet tall. He's six feet. And I don't think he's exactly going to be down with your plan for the evening, Wren."

Everyone passing is slowing their steps to listen, looking over their shoulders at the two of us, and I can't help the furious zing of power that slams a locker shut two doors down. A freshman girl jumps back with a gasp and shoots me a strange look as she hurries down the hall.

But before I can say anything else, another hand on my shoulder startles me, and I find Jess there, Darcia beside her. They're glowering, and Jess lets her voice carry when she says, "I think she told you to drop it, new boy. What part of that didn't you understand?"

Across the hall, Yuri Fiske snickers, but Gabriel just rolls his eyes. "You actually don't know anything about this, so . . ." He spreads his hands as if this explains everything, and for a minute I actually feel sorry for him.

"What I know is that my friend is telling you to leave her alone, and you're not listening," Jess says steadily, and Gabriel might not understand what it means when she gets that calm, but I do, and so does Darcia. She actually swallows and takes a step back, although I'm pretty sure Jess won't take a swing at him. "I also know that guys with testosterone poisoning are gross, and need to walk away and go lift metaphorical weights somewhere that is completely else."

A few lockers down, Sera Fine and Jilli Beckett clap. Yuri grins, leaning against the opposite wall and looking Jess up and down like he wants to eat her for lunch, which is gross, but whatever.

"Wren," Gabriel says, and I can't tell if it's a warning or a plea, but I don't really care at the moment.

"I'm doing this," I tell him, standing up straight and looking him directly in the eye. I know speculation about what "this" is will be all over school in less than ten minutes, as well as hotly discussed between Jess and Dar, but I don't care about that, either. It's not like anyone will ever guess. "And I *don't want* your help, not this time."

I don't want it to mean good-bye, but it's up to Gabriel to decide how to interpret it. I have to say good-bye to the first boy I ever loved tonight, for real this time. If I'm still standing by the time it's done, I'll be relieved.

But as I walk away, locker and books forgotten, the outrage in my chest is already melting because Jess and Dar are right behind me.

CHAPTER TWENTY-FIVE

MOM DOESN'T QUESTION ME GOING OUT later that night, and I don't try to hide it. She's still up watching TV, and when I tell her that I have one last thing to take care of, she just looks at me for a long moment before nodding.

"Be careful?"

"I know," I say. "I will."

She pushes hair off her forehead and takes a deep breath. "Back to whatever passes for normal after this?"

I shrug. There's normal and then there's normal, and then there's the big question mark of my father still lingering between us, punctuating the one thing I still need an answer to. "We can try?"

I know she knows all of that. It's there in the tilt of her head, her clear, warm eyes. "I'm willing if you are. School tomorrow, remember."

When I shut the door behind me to walk to Gabriel's, I almost feel good.

Almost. Because now I have to see Gabriel, and after our confrontation in the hall earlier, my feelings for him are snarled so messily, I'm not sure they're ever coming untangled. I never knew you could want to curl up on a boy's lap at the same time you wanted to hit him really hard on the head until he got a clue.

I'm not even processing what will come after I leave Gabriel's apartment, not yet. It's too big, a mountain of grief and regret and more than a little fear, and I figure it's probably better to climb it when the time comes rather than imagine climbing it now.

I know Mom reminded me about school, but I'm pretty sure I won't be getting out of bed tomorrow unless someone uses a cattle prod. And, like, a rocket launcher for backup.

It's cold and clear as I walk, and the moon is just as full as promised, a cool silver coin laid on the dark cloth of the sky. I huddle into my coat as I turn the corner onto Gabriel's block, breathing in the smokiness of dry leaves and dying earth, and center all my power in my chest, where I can feel it.

I asked Mom about it after dinner. Robin had gone up to her room, and I was clearing the plates from the table.

"How do you . . . focus?" I said, and turned around to face her. She was frowning. "The power, I mean. How do you keep it under control?"

For a moment, I was sure she was either going to explode or turtle up the way she always used to. Instead, she stood there with a dish of leftover rice in one hand and studied my face.

"There's not a simple answer to that, babe," she said finally, and put the bowl in the fridge before coming to stand next to me. "It depends on what you want to do."

I couldn't think of anything to say to that, because there was no way I was going to explain why I needed my power to be completely under control tonight.

When I didn't answer, she tilted her head sideways and bit her bottom lip. "It's a matter of wanting something enough, I guess. Being able to clear your mind of everything else and concentrate specifically on making something happen." She glanced at the kitchen table and scowled. Robin's cat was standing there, licking a plate very delicately. "Like this."

She drew in a deep, slow breath and looked at the cat, very steadily, and for a second I swore her eyes got darker, deeper. She raised her right hand slowly, palm up, and the next thing I knew the cat was levitating over the table, eyes wide, hissing.

She set him down with a little bit of a *thunk*, and smirked. "Is that what you mean?"

I couldn't help laughing, and for a second it all poured out—surprise, fear, love, grief. I probably sounded a little hysterical. But I managed to nod. "Yeah, sort of."

It wasn't really all I needed to know, but it helped. I'd been doing it ever since, concentrating, focusing, letting myself feel the power inside, smoothing it into a tight, neat ball with no rough edges, no jagged pieces. I want to be able to throw it exactly where I need it to go.

I'm as ready as I'm ever going to be by the time I climb the stairs to Gabriel's apartment. I have to be. Time's up after tonight, at least for another month, and that's not even on the same planet as possible.

Gabriel answers the door after I knock once, softly. It's eleven o'clock, and despite the muted hum of a TV I can hear in the apartment downstairs, it seems dangerous to break the night stillness.

"Hey." He stands back to let me in, and slips my backpack from my shoulder as I walk past. It's heavy with everything I need, and I don't mind the gesture, since he just sets it on the table by the door. "So."

Awkward isn't even the word for the moment, although he seems to have accepted that I'm taking Danny to the graveyard and doing this thing on my own. He's not bristling anymore, anyway, and I'm grateful for that.

He leans against the wall, hands jammed in the pockets of his jeans, and I can't help thinking it makes him look like he's trying to keep himself from reaching out to touch me. I cram the small part of me that wants that into a box and hide it deep in the back of my head. I have to.

"Are you ready?"

I want to say *I hope so*, because that's the raw truth, but instead I nod, as slow and as calm as I can. "I am." I can stop lying for good tomorrow.

"How are you going to get him over there?"

"I have a spell."

He nods, and his hair falls into his eyes as he looks at the floor. His feet are bare, long and pale beneath his jeans legs, and they're so naked, so vulnerable, I melt a little.

"I worked on the spell all last night and this afternoon. It's pretty good, I think. I mean, as good as something like this can be, considering what it's supposed to do. And I have everything I need."

He looks up halfway through my impromptu little speech, startled, but by the end he's nodding along, and it's not clear even to me who I'm supposed to be reassuring.

"Explain it to me?"

So I do, sitting on the sofa facing him, our bent knees touching. It's good to talk it through one last time, and with every step I can feel how right it is, all the pieces sliding together with a series of neat clicks.

"Can I tell you to be careful?" he says when I'm done. He bumps his knee against mine. "Or are you going to slug me?"

I bump back, and smile. "I'm not going to hit you." I swallow, gathering the right words the way I gathered all the elements for the spell. "But I do want you to know, I'm doing this alone because I have to. I did this . . . thing. And no one can fix it but me. No one should fix it but me. I have all this power and I have to figure out how to use it. You can't change that. And you can't really help me with it, either. And I'm not doing this for you, but . . . I would like to think you've got my back, just like Jess and Dar did today."

The apartment is silent except for the distant hum of the refrigerator and the soft rush of wheels on the street outside. For a moment, Gabriel is as still as Danny, his gray eyes fixed steadily on my face, unmoving.

And I want so much to study them, sometime after tonight, to see what they're like when he's laughing, or when he's about to kiss me, or when he's falling asleep, or reading something he can't put down. I want to know him the way I knew Danny, inside and out, and it's scary. No, it's terrifying, because the last time I let myself do that, I ended up down some rabbit hole where I drank from every bottle and never once thought about the consequences, just so I could cling to something that wasn't only mine.

Love is the ultimate two-way street. I'm just a little nervous about getting behind the wheel again.

"All I want is for you to be okay," he says finally, and I have to lean forward to catch each word because his voice is pitched so low. "Actually, no, that's a lie. That's not all I want. But it's the first thing. It's just . . . I like to fix things. And when you can see inside someone, when you know what they need, it's hard not to give it to them. Like my mom, when she was dying. All she wanted was for my dad to tell her this one thing, to make this one promise to her." He pauses to clear his throat, and even though I want more than anything to reach out and take his hand, I just wait for him to finish. I can't help him with this any more than he can help me with Danny.

When he opens his mouth again, his voice is even rougher. "And my dad didn't know that. He never would have thought of it, and she wasn't going to ask. But *I* knew. And that meant that I could tell him. And even though he lied to her, she heard him say what she needed him to say before she died."

That's . . . horrible. Horrible and sad and not something I ever want to happen between me and someone I love. But it's also not really what's happening here.

"I'm so sorry." I press my knee harder into his, and he gives me a tight smile. "But . . . if you really looked, and I'm guessing you at least tried, you know that I don't secretly want you to go all superhero and do my dirty work for me, right?"

His smile is a little warmer now, but I think it would probably taste bittersweet if I pressed my mouth to his. "Yeah, I do. And I think that's what's really tough to swallow. Being helpless sort of sucks, Wren."

The surprised snort that escapes makes us both laugh a little. "I get that, believe me."

Gabriel glances at his watch. "It's almost eleven twenty. You should probably start the show, you know?"

I do. I take a deep breath and get up off the couch,

and when I turn around, Olivia is there.

"I only listened a little." She shrugs, but then she crosses the room to put her arms around me. "Good luck seems like a crazy thing to say, so I'm just going to say do your thing, kid. I'm sorry you have to."

I let her hold me for a second, my nose buried in her hair, but then I push away. I can't waste time now. Gabriel squeezes my hand and kisses me, but I have to give him credit—after I go into his room, he disappears. He doesn't ask to watch me as I whisper the words to get Danny to his feet, and he doesn't watch as I lead him out of the apartment and down the street, his steps carefully measured as he walks beside me, his hand in mine.

This time is for me, to say good-bye to Danny. And I can't help but be thankful that this docile, silent boy is the one beside me, because if I had to face the Danny I remember, the one I fell in love with, right now, I'm not sure I could do what I have to.

CHAPTER TWENTY-SIX

IT'S APRIL, AND IT'S RAINING, THE KIND OF gray, sliding, icy rain that won't stop, until everything feels damp and clammy, even the curtains when I pull them shut against the slicked window.

Danny is warm. His soaked jacket is downstairs on the coatrack, and even though his hair is wet against the back of his neck, even though he has to rub his chilly hands together for a few minutes to get the blood pumping into them, when I run my hands up under his shirt, his back is warm. When I rest my cheek against his chest, nuzzling into the faded cotton, he's warm. I want to wrap myself in him. And I'm going to. Right now, this minute, I know that.

My mom is at work, and Robin is at a weekend soccer camp upstate, and I don't know where Danny's mom thinks he is, but it doesn't matter. It's Saturday and it's just noon, and no one is going to be looking for us for hours.

We haven't talked about this, not in so many words. I'm not even sure Danny knows what I'm thinking. But we've been edging closer to it for weeks, months, and there aren't a lot of boundaries left between us when we're tangled up together anymore.

I want to erase them all, finally. I want. . . . That's as far as I think, really. I just *want*.

"Wren?"

My name is muffled, because I'm kissing him, but I'm also pulling him down onto the bed, unbuttoning the flannel he's got over an old Weezer shirt. I'm about four steps ahead of him, and I need to let him catch up.

I drag in a shaky breath and kneel beside him on the bed, running my thumb over his cheekbone. I don't know what he can see in my eyes, but he blinks and says, "Yeah?"

I nod. "Yeah."

"But I don't, um, I don't have—"

"I do." The condoms Mom bought me—and God,

I am *never* telling him that—are in my bedside drawer. "We're all set."

"Oh yeah?" He cocks an eyebrow, pulls me off balance and into his lap. "What if I say no? Ever think about that, Miss I'm All Set?"

"I really hope you're kidding." I kiss his collarbone, the smooth slope of his shoulder where it arches into his neck.

"I don't think you have to worry," he says, and the words tickle my ear as his tongue paints a light stripe against my cheek.

We don't talk after that, not really. And it's not perfect, I mean, there aren't, like, rainbows and fireworks and sirens going off, but it's perfect anyway. Because it's Danny almost toppling over when he wrestles out of his jeans, and it's Danny laughing into the skin of my belly when I hit my head on the wall hard enough that we both hear it crack. And it's Danny who tangles our fingers together when we're finally there, holding on tight, watching my face, and it's Danny who lets me touch and explore and whisper and press smiling kisses into his hair and his cheek later, after.

I hope he remembers it the way I do. Or that he remembered it that way before I gave him memories he was never meant to have.

He's quiet beside me in the dark cemetery, although he does trace his name on the stone that marks the head of his grave. I don't know how much he understands about what's going to happen, and I don't want to tell him. The spell I cast when he was still lying on Gabriel's bed was written to make him mobile, but not much more. He's awake, but he's not, not really—the boy I loved is buried somewhere in a body that looks familiar, but isn't really the most important part of him.

That Danny, the one who used to chase me down the street, threatening to tickle me if I didn't kiss him again, who used to piggyback me up and down the science hall after school as we left the building, who used to sing snatches of songs to me on the phone when we were both home in bed at night, he's been gone for a long time. He's the one I'm never really going to be okay with losing, but at least now I know that isn't up to me.

At five minutes to midnight, I arrange him on the grave, laying him down gently, and he doesn't protest. He watches me, his eyes dark and blank, and blinks a little when I bend over to kiss him and a tear falls on his cheek.

"I need you to close your eyes now, and listen to my voice." I press the words against his cold mouth, and I can't believe my voice is steady. My heart is beating so hard and fast it's a little frightening, but nothing's changed otherwise—I can still feel the power coiled taut and ready inside me.

I trim a lock of his hair and he doesn't move. I squeeze his hand before I draw my athame across it, and he still doesn't flinch. The blood is as cold and sluggish as he is, gleaming nearly black in the moonlight. I smear it onto a picture of him, one of my favorites, and press his hair into it before I check my watch.

One minute left.

I kneel at his feet and lay the picture between his calves on the patch of earth where I've pulled the grass away. One handful of dirt and the picture is covered, Danny's huge grin and laughing eyes obscured. I swallow thickly and start to chant, the blade poised in my right hand and my power cresting high and eager in my chest.

> *Tonight I call Death to embrace this boy*
> *Tonight I seek peace for him*
> *From ash he emerged, and to ash he returns.*
>
> *Spirits bright*
> *Spirits dark*
> *Spirits undecided and in between*
> *Witness my invocation.*

To Death you return, Danny.
Peace awaits you.
Life has no hold on you anymore.

By candlelight
By starlight
By moonlight growing stronger
I command this to be.

With this symbol of Danny
With his blood
I command this to be.

Find Death, Danny.
Find peace.
Find Death, Danny.
Find peace.

I don't realize how hard I'm crying until I open my eyes as wind shudders over the ground, a flapping sheet of it, and the candle flickers out.

Danny is gone.

I'm not sure how long I lie there, my face, muddy with tears now, pressed to the cold dirt. I feel hollow inside, scooped dry by the time I sit up. Despite that, I know what's different now, what I didn't realize the last time I was here, chanting under the moon.

My power is still where I put it, neatly rolled into a ball and balanced at my center. Before, it raged through me like a flood, washing into every nerve, every vein, completely unchecked.

Now, I can decide when to use it, if I use it.

It's a cold comfort, but I'll take it for now. I'm shaky when I stand up, and I put everything away in my bag, except for the picture of Danny, which I hold up and light. I let it burn down to my fingers, and then I say good-bye and let go as the ashes flutter to Danny's grave.

What I feel most, as I pick my way through the headstones toward the gate, is alone. I think it's what I was scared of when Danny died, or one of the things, anyway. It's just as cold a feeling as I imagined.

Except when I walk through the gates, hitching my backpack more securely over my shoulder and wiping away the last tears with the back of one dirty hand, I see Gabriel. He's across the street, leaning against a mailbox, a paper cup from the mini-mart in one hand. He doesn't wave, he doesn't smile, and he doesn't walk toward me.

He waits.

And I think that this is what I would like love to be. Leaving room for each other, knowing that not every step is going to be side by side.

Giving more than taking. Waiting. Trusting.

I cross the street and reach for his hand. He lets me take it, squeezing my fingers briefly.

"Walk me home?" I ask him.

He hands me the cup, hot sweet tea, offers to take my bag. I let him, watching as the weight of it pulls down his shoulder.

And then we walk together in the moonlight, hand in hand, until I'm home.

AUTHOR'S NOTE

MY ZOMBIE, SUCH AS HE IS, ISN'T GEORGE Romero's, as you probably figured out. He's closer to the kind of zombie you might create with Haitian vodou magic, a corpse reanimated and then controlled by a sorcerer. That said, with a few minor exceptions, almost everything in this book is straight out of my imagination. I took liberties with the geography of the town where I went to high school, and made up a bunch of stuff out of whole cloth because in fiction, that's allowed, for which I'm grateful. Resemblances to any people living, dead, or undead are only a coincidence, except for the Brobecks' song "Visitation of the Ghost," which I adore.

ACKNOWLEDGMENTS

MANY THANKS TO THE PEOPLE WHO KEEP ME sane, and love me even when I'm not. Lee, for all kinds of excellent cheerleading and general awesomeness; Donna, for making me laugh and letting me talk through scenes with her; Jilli and Bev, for reading and shaking their pom-poms, and helping with incantations; ita, for listening to me whine and distracting me with Winchesters; Maureen, for believing I could do this, and encouraging me all the way; and Erica, for getting it and loving it and making it a thousand times better.